PURRFECT ALIBI

THE MYSTERIES OF MAX 9

NIC SAINT

PUSS IN PRINT PUBLICATIONS

PURRFECT ALIBI

The Mysteries of Max 9

Copyright © 2019 by Nic Saint

Edited by Chereese Graves

www.nicsaint.com

Give feedback on the book at: info@nicsaint.com

facebook.com/nicsaintauthor
@nicsaintauthor

First Edition

Printed in the U.S.A

PROLOGUE

*M*arge Poole surveyed the scene. She wondered if they'd set out enough chairs. The event she was staging was without a doubt the biggest and most ambitious one she'd ever taken on. Even though the Hampton Cove library had been remodeled five years ago with exactly this kind of literary event in mind, and a small conference room had been added for writers to hold readings, Marge had never expected ever to land the bestselling thriller writer in the world for one of her Author of the Month evenings.

But there he was. Chris Ackerman. Author of such bestsellers as *The Connor Conundrum* and *The Dixon Dilemma*. America's favorite writer and the most-borrowed author of all time. The scribe was seated on the small stage, peering through his reading glasses and going over his notes, an expensive-looking golden fountain pen poised in his hand. When he noticed Marge nervously bustling about, he fixed his pale blue eyes on her.

"Wasn't Burke supposed to be here by now?" he asked.

There was an edge to his voice, and Marge didn't wonder. A long-standing feud between Chris Ackerman and Rockwell Burke, the well-known horror novelist, had existed ever since Burke had announced that he felt Ackerman's books were the work of a hack and a dilettante and had discounted his prose as bad writing. In fact it had surprised Marge a great deal when Burke had accepted to host the evening, and interview Ackerman on stage.

Perhaps the horrormeister had had a change of heart. More likely, though, it was because his own once flourishing career had hit a snag, his last three books not selling as well as he'd hoped, at which point his publisher must have insisted he try to turn things around by associating himself with the reigning king of the *New York Times* bestseller list.

"He'll be here," Marge assured Ackerman, who was glancing at his watch.

"He'd better," grumbled the famous writer. In his early seventies now, Chris Ackerman was a ruddy-faced heavyset man with a quiet air of self-confidence. "If he doesn't show up I'll have to tell the audience what I really think of him." He chuckled. "That his best years are behind him, and that I hated every book he's put out for the past decade."

"You don't really mean that," said Marge, shocked at the harsh words.

"Oh, but I do," said Ackerman, adjusting his glasses to owlishly stare at Marge. "My publisher told me not to engage, but if Burke stands me up all bets are off." He wagged a finger. "I'll bet he's doing it on purpose. Promising to make nice then making a fool of me."

"I'm sure he's simply delayed," said Marge, checking the door to the left of the stage. "His publicist would have told me if Mr. Burke had decided to cancel at the last minute."

"Not unless he wants to make a fool of me," Ackerman repeated.

Marge checked her own watch. One hour until showtime. There was still plenty of time for Rockwell Burke to show up. Then again, the man's publicist had promised Marge he'd be there on time, so he could go over some of the questions with Ackerman.

Marge, a fine-boned fifty-something woman with long blond hair, chewed her lip and walked the short distance between the conference room and the library proper. She wondered if she'd unlocked the front doors. It worried her that no one had shown up yet. Usually when she organized her Author of the Month evenings at least a few people arrived early, wanting to secure a good seat—or an autograph from the featured author. And with Chris Ackerman as the featured speaker she'd expected the town to turn out en masse.

The Hampton Cove library wasn't a big operation. In fact it was downright modest. But it had a nice selection of books, DVDs and CDs, a computer room where users could surf the Internet, a cozy kids' corner with a pirate ship where the kids could sit and read, a colorful fish tank, a collection of stuffed animals, and cheerful artwork by a local artist.

Breezing past the checkout desk and the newspaper stand, she quickly moved to the door, where her husband and her mother stood peering out at the courtyard in front of the library. The size of a postage stamp, the courtyard nevertheless featured a fountain and a few stone benches. At this very moment, though, it was as deserted as the library itself.

"Where is everyone?" asked Marge.

Vesta Muffin, a septuagenarian the spitting image of Estelle Getty, lifted her bony shoulders. "Probably at home watching *The Bachelor*. Which is what I would be doing right now if you hadn't roped me into this meet and greet with your childhood crush."

"He was never my crush," said Marge, checking the doors

to see if they weren't locked. They weren't. "I just like his books, that's all. He's an amazing writer."

"I like him," Tex said. A buff man with a shock of white hair, Tex always kept a Chris Ackerman on his bedside table so he could read a couple of chapters before going to sleep.

"Too bloodthirsty for my taste," said Gran, adjusting her large, horn-rimmed glasses. "All those serial killers and crazy maniacs. How many serial killers do people really think are out there? Give me EL James any day over your creepy Chuck Peckerwood."

"Chris Ackerman."

"Huh?"

"Chris Ackerman, not Chuck Peckerwood."

"Whatever. I'm just saying. If there really were as many serial killers as Ackerwood wants us to believe, the streets would be crawling with them and we'd all be dead right now, murdered in the most gruesome way possible."

"It's fiction, Mom. It's not supposed to be real."

"EL James is real. Christian Grey is out there. In fact the world is full of Christian Greys. Only problem is the world is also full of Anastasia Steeles who hog all the Christian Greys and leave nothing for the rest of us shlubs."

Tex chuckled. "I doubt billionaires are anything like Christian Grey," he said. "Real billionaires don't look like runway models. They look like Bill Gates or Warren Buffett."

"How would you know?" said Vesta. "You're not a billionaire."

Tex agreed that he wasn't. Still, he said, he believed Christian Grey to be just as fictitious as Chris Ackerman's trademark serial killers.

Marge didn't think Christian Grey, real or not, would fancy a crusty old lady with tiny white curls and a big attitude problem. But since she didn't want to get drawn into the argument, she decided to keep her comments to herself.

"I don't get it. Last month we had Jacqueline Rose Garner and people showed up an hour before the start of the event."

"Which just goes to show you people are fed up with murder and mayhem. They want love and passion. Speaking of which, did you know Chase asked Odelia out on a date?"

"Yes, she told me. Chase took her to Villa Frank. Too bad it's tonight. She really wanted to be here so she could meet Chris and Rockwell Burke."

"You can't beat love," said Vesta in uncharacteristically sentimental fashion.

"He took her to Villa Frank, huh?" said Tex, rocking back on his heels. "I took Marge there for our wedding anniversary. Remember, honey? You loved their steak pizzaiola."

"Oh, I did. And how about that almond joy sundae? That was to die for."

For the next forty-five minutes, conversation flowed back and forth, mainly focusing on Tex and Marge's daughter Odelia and Odelia's boyfriend Chase Kingsley. People finally started showing up, though they were in no great hurry to take their seats, instead opting to chat with friends and acquaintances. For most people these Author of the Month evenings were more an excuse to socialize than to come and listen to an author read from their work.

Just then, there was a soft yelp coming from the conference room. Marge immediately whipped her head around. She listened for a moment, but when no other sounds came, she relaxed again. "I better go and see if Burke has arrived yet," she said.

"I'll come with you," said Tex.

"No, you better stay here and welcome the guests," said Marge.

She retraced her steps to the conference room. Chris Ackerman was still where she'd left him, seated in his chair on stage. Only he seemed to have fallen asleep, his notes having dropped from his hands and scattered all around him on the floor. Oh, my.

"Mr. Ackerman?" she said, threading a path through the chairs. "Are you all right?"

Even from ten feet away she could see the star of the evening wasn't all right at all. The first sign that something was amiss were the drops of a dark crimson substance splattered on the sheets of paper on the floor. Even before it dawned on her what those drops represented, her eyes fixed on a strange object protruding from the writer's neck.

It was the golden fountain pen, its nib now deeply embedded into the man's neck.

The world's bestselling writer... was dead.

CHAPTER 1

*O*delia Poole, star reporter for the Hampton Cove Gazette, wasn't used to being wined and dined in quite this fashion. Chase Kingsley, her boyfriend and local cop with the Hampton Cove Police Department, hadn't just taken her to any old place. Ever since he'd asked her out, he'd been highly secretive about the itinerary for their date, and only when he'd picked her up in his squad car and entered the Villa Frank parking lot had she caught on that this wasn't going to be a quick burger at the local diner but an actual fancy date.

Good thing she'd dressed up for the occasion, her off-the-shoulder red pencil dress pretty much the fanciest thing she had hanging in her closet. She'd bought it on the instigation of her mother, who insisted she have at least one nice thing to wear for galas, movie premieres, chamber of commerce banquets or the occasional fancy reception. Her usual costume consisting of jeans, T-shirt and a sweater the dress made her feel slightly self-conscious, especially since there was some bust involved. Watching Chase's jaw drop when he'd come to pick her up had been more than enough to dispel those qualms, though.

"You look lovely," he said, not for the first time.

"You don't look so bad yourself," she purred.

That was an understatement. Chase, usually a jeans-and-check shirt man himself, had gone all out as well, dressing up in an actual tux for the occasion. His long dark brown hair was combed back from his brow, his square jaw was entirely free of stubble, and his muscular frame filled out that tux to the extent that Odelia had no trouble picturing what he looked like underneath. Then again, the man was no stranger to her bed. Or at least he hadn't been until her grandmother had decided to move in and cramp his style.

But now that Gran had moved out again, the coast was clear, and it was obvious that Chase intended to move in on a more permanent basis—possibly the whole reason for splashing on a night at Villa Frank, one of the more posh places in Hampton Cove.

She took a sip from her wine and felt her head spin. It was more the way Chase was looking at her right now than the alcohol, though, his green-specked blue eyes holding a promise that she hoped he intended to keep.

"So what movie have you picked?" she asked.

"I thought I'd go with a golden oldie. *Bringing Up Baby*."

"Ooh! I love Katherine Hepburn."

"What about Cary Grant?"

"He's fine, I guess," she said with a coquettish flutter of her lashes. In fact he was more than fine. Cary Grant had always been one of her favorite actors. More than today's movie heroes, he had charm, style and charisma and that elusive *je-ne-sais-quoi*.

"Phew. I hoped you'd like my selection."

"I love it." She didn't mention that she'd already seen the movie about a dozen times on TCM. On the big screen it would look even better, of course. Their local movie theater was holding a screwball comedy retrospective and she was happy Chase was a fan, too.

"So what do you think is Cary Grant's best movie?" she asked now.

He pressed his napkin to his lips. Their menu had consisted of shrimp scampi and lobster stuffed flounder with a side of pasta and marinara sauce and brickle for dessert: toasted almonds, ice cream and whipped cream. A real feast. And the evening wasn't over yet. Not by a long shot.

"I like the Hitchcocks best," Chase said. *"North by Northwest, To Catch a Thief, Charade..."*

"Charade isn't a Hitchcock," she told him. "It's Stanley Donen's Hitchcock homage."

Chase grinned. "Of course you would know that, Miss Movie Buff."

"I like *Arsenic and Old Lace*. Oh, and *Mr. Blandings Builds His Dream House*, of course."

"Huh. I thought you'd have gone for the more romantic ones."

"I guess I'm a funny girl at heart," she quipped.

"Yes, you are," he said, and gave her one of those looks that made her melt like the toffee-flavored ice cream on her tongue. "Not only funny but smart, beautiful, compassionate…"

Her cheeks flushed, and not just from the fireplace they were sitting close to. "Keep this up and I just might let you get frisky through the second act of *Bringing Up Baby*."

"Oh, I'm counting on it."

She dug her spoon into the caramel-colored ice cream. "Is it just me or is it hot in here?"

Chase cleared his throat. "I heard your grandmother moved back in with your parents?"

And there it was: the reason he'd asked her out on a date

in the first place. Or at least that's what she hoped. They'd been going out for months now, and it was time to put their budding relationship on a more permanent footing. Since Chase bunked with Odelia's uncle, having not had much luck renting a place of his own in town, moving in with her was the logical thing to do. And oh boy was she ready. And she'd just opened her mouth to confirm that her grandmother had, indeed, moved back in with her folks when both of their phones started to sing in unison.

"Huh," said Chase with a frown. "It's your uncle."

"My mom," said Odelia with a smile, and tapped the green Accept icon. "Hey, Mom. What's up?" When the garbled words of her mother flowed into her ear, though, her smile quickly vanished. "Wow, slow down. What are you talking about?"

"He's dead!" Mom practically shouted into the phone. "Chris Ackerman is dead and now they think he may have been murdered and that I had something to do with it!"

As her mother explained what happened, Odelia fixed her gaze on Chase, whose jaw was clenching while he listened to what Uncle Alec, the town's chief of police, had to say.

Looked like Cary Grant and Katherine Hepburn would have to take a rain check.

CHAPTER 2

I won't conceal I was having a tough time at it. To be honest I don't think I'm cut out to be a teacher, and teaching a bunch of unruly cats was definitely not my idea of an evening well spent.

"We'll watch it again until you discover when Aurora picked up the all-important and vital clue," I said, and tapped the rewind button on the TV's remote. When my audience groaned loudly, I added, "And no buts. If we're going to do this, we need to do it right."

"But, Max!" Brutus cried. "We've seen this movie three times already!"

"And we'll see it three times more if that's what it takes," I said stubbornly.

"*The Bachelor* is on," said Harriet. "I love *The Bachelor*. Can't we watch that instead?"

I gave her a stern-faced look. "No, we can't. *The Bachelor* won't teach us the things we need to know as cat sleuths. Aurora Teagarden will."

Unfortunately Odelia had only taped one Aurora Teagarden movie, even though I'd asked her to tape all of them if she had the chance. Instead, she'd taped a movie called *I'll Be Home for Christmas*. Which featured a dog, and as everyone knows, no cat wants to be seen dead watching dogs on TV—or in real life, for that matter—so that was a definite no-no. Besides, there was no mystery, only a silly romance plot and a lot of tinsel.

I watched the screen intently, then paused the movie just when Aurora opened her mouth to say something, her face a mask of concentration. "See? This is the moment she realizes who the killer is. See the way her forehead crinkles? How her eyebrows draw up?"

"She looks constipated," said Harriet, tapping her paw against Odelia's leather couch.

"Do I look like that when I get an idea, Max?" asked Dooley.

"You would if you ever got an idea," said Brutus with a grin.

"I get ideas," said Dooley. "I get ideas all the time. Just now I got the idea that Odelia's been gone a long time, and that I hope she'll be home soon."

"That's great, Dooley," I said. "But that's not the kind of idea we're talking about."

"So tell us exactly what we are talking about, Max," said Brutus as he suppressed a yawn. Even though he, unlike Harriet, wasn't a big fan of *The Bachelor*, it was obvious he wasn't remotely interested in my lecture on modern sleuthing techniques either.

"We're talking about being perceptive," I said. "About not missing even the teensiest, tiniest clue. For all we know a cigarette butt can lead us to the killer. Or, as in this case…" I pointed to the screen. "Pizza boxes tucked underneath the kitchen sink."

"Are the pizza boxes a very important clue, Max?" asked Dooley eagerly.

"They are," said Brutus before I could respond. "They're a clue to this couple's eating habits. It tells us that they like pizza." He was grinning again, clearly enjoying himself.

"The pizza boxes tell us that these people took the missing students hostage," I said, directing a censorious look at Brutus. "It tells Aurora—and the viewer—that the missing students are, in fact, somewhere in the house. So yes, Dooley, the pizza boxes are a very important clue. They're that all-important, telling a-ha type of clue you want to find."

"Pizza boxes," Dooley repeated reverently, as if memorizing the words.

"They're an important clue in *this* particular case," I hastened to add. "In any other case they're probably completely irrelevant."

Dooley looked confused. "So... pizza boxes aren't *always* a clue?"

"No, they're not. It all depends on the circumstances. In this case the pizza boxes—"

"Oh, enough about the pizza boxes already!" Harriet cried, lifting her paws in a gesture of despair. "Can we watch *The Bachelor* now? I'll bet Jock's dinner with LaRue is still in full swing. We just might catch dessert if you turn off this Aurora nonsense right now."

"I think I need to see it one more time," said Dooley. "I think I missed something."

Harriet looked as if she was ready to pounce on Dooley, but restrained herself with a supreme effort. "What don't you get, Dooley?" she asked instead in clipped tones.

Dooley was shaking his head confusedly. "Well, it's those pizza boxes. I don't see how Aurora goes from seeing the empty pizza boxes to finding those missing students."

"God give me strength," Harriet muttered, very expressively rolling her eyes.

"Why don't you let us do the thinking from now on, Dooley?" Brutus suggested.

"You think so?" said Dooley.

"Yes, unlike you I do think. In fact I think so much I don't mind doing a little thinking for you, too, so that you can..." He gave Dooley a dubious look. "Do whatever it is you do."

"I could... help you search for those pizza boxes," said Dooley hopefully.

"You do that," said Brutus, patting the other cat on the shoulder. "You do that."

I now realize I may have committed the ultimate faux-pas. I've neglected to introduce you to my merry band of felines. Let me rectify that right now, by introducing myself first. My name is Max, and I'm Odelia Poole's feisty feline sidekick. I'm strapping, I'm blorange, and I'm proud to be of assistance to my human, who's probably one of the finest humans a cat could ever hope to be associated with. She also stems from a long line of females who can converse with felines, which makes her an honorary feline in my book.

The three cats lounging on the couch are (reading from left to right) Dooley, who's a gray Ragamuffin and my side-kick (yes, he's a sidekick's sidekick), Brutus, a black muscle-head who likes to think he's the bee's knees (or more appropriately the cat's whiskers) and finally we have Harriet, who's by way of being Brutus's mate. She's also a pretty, prissy Persian but don't tell her I said that because she can be quite catty. And she has some very sharp claws.

"I think I saw a pizza box yesterday, Max," Dooley said now, showing the kind of zeal and initiative a feline sleuth worth their salt should strive for. "If you want I can show you."

"That's all right, Dooley," I said. "We can go into that when we start the practical part of this introductory training."

"Practical part?" asked Harriet. "There's a practical part?"

"Of course there is," I said. "First we learn the basics, then we apply them to a real-world situation."

"I still don't get why you get to teach this course, Max," said Brutus. "What makes you think you're qualified?"

"I'll have you know I've solved quite a number of high-profile cases," I told him.

"You couldn't have pulled those off without me and you know it. In fact before I arrived in town you hadn't solved a single case. Not a one. Admit it, Max."

I was puffing out my chest to give him a proper rebuke when all of a sudden there was a commotion at the door. It flew open and Odelia burst in.

"I need you guys to come with me," she said, panting as if she'd just run a marathon. "There's been a murder." She fixed us with a meaningful look. "My mom is implicated."

CHAPTER 3

"So what happened?" I asked.

"I have no idea," said Odelia.

"So who did it?" asked Dooley.

"I have no idea."

"So who's the victim?" asked Harriet.

"I have no idea!"

After this rare outburst, we all sat silent for a moment. Not for very long, though. We are cats, after all, not church mice. You can't keep a good cat down. Or quiet.

"So what do you want us to do?" I asked.

Odelia, who was visibly overwrought at the thought of her mother being involved in some dreadful murder business, heaved a deep sigh and rolled her shoulders in a bid to relax them. She'd been sitting hunched over the steering wheel, which I could have told her was the kind of posture that could lead to some serious neck trouble. "I want you to talk to any animal you can find within a mile radius of the library. If anyone out there saw something I want to know about it. If someone out there heard something I want to know about it. And if someone out there so much as smelled something, I want—"

"Let me guess," I said. "You want to know about it."

She didn't smile. "This is my mother we're talking about, Max."

"I understand," I said. "And we'll do everything in our power to—"

"So did Marge kill someone?" asked Dooley.

It wasn't the right question to ask, so when Odelia's head snapped around, for a moment I thought she was going to bite Dooley's head straight off. Instead, she merely snapped, "Of course she didn't kill someone. My mother is the sweetest, kindest woman I know. She wouldn't hurt a fly, let alone the bestselling thriller writer on the planet."

"I saw her swat a fly once," said Dooley conversationally. "It was a big fly. One of those blue ones. Made a big mess, too."

When I gave him a prod in the ribs he blinked and turned to me, looking slightly offended. "Shut up," I loud-whispered.

"What did I say?"

Raising my voice, I said, "If anyone saw, heard, smelled or tasted something, we'll find them and let you know, Odelia."

Odelia grunted something I understood to be approval, and continued staring straight ahead through the windshield, while her foot ground the accelerator into the floorboard and the car flew across the road at a rate of speed which was frankly disconcerting, not to mention frowned upon by traffic police everywhere.

"So who *is* the bestselling thriller on the planet?" asked Harriet.

When Odelia didn't respond, Brutus decided to do the honors. "Agatha Christie, of course," he said. "In fact she's the best-selling author of all time. Sold billions of books."

"Agatha Christie died years ago," I said.

"So?"

"So she can't have been murdered tonight if she's been dead for years."

This stumped him for a moment. He quickly rallied, though. "Maybe she didn't die. Maybe she only pretended to die but she's been alive all this time only to be murdered at Marge's library tonight."

"Agatha Christie was almost ninety years old when she died," I said.

"So?"

"This was years ago! She would have been a hundred-whatever!"

"So? Humans get very old. Hundreds of years, probably. Maybe even thousands."

For a long time I'd been laboring under the same misapprehension. I'd always figured Odelia was probably a couple of hundred years old. But she'd recently cured me of this mistaken belief in the longevity of the human species. Odelia, as it turned out, wasn't even thirty years old yet. And most humans never made it past the age of a hundred. Weird, huh?

"Trust me, Brutus. Whoever was killed tonight, it wasn't Agatha Christie."

"Chris Ackerman," said Odelia suddenly.

"Who?" asked Dooley.

"Chris Ackerman. The thriller writer?"

Neither me nor Brutus, Harriet or Dooley showed any signs of recognition. Then again, cats are not your great readers. We love television—mostly cat food commercials—but we lack the patience and the attention span to read page after page like humans do.

"So who was this Chris Ackerman?" I asked.

"Like I said. A thriller writer."

"Any good?" asked Harriet.

"I liked him," said Odelia. "He was the master of the cliffhanger."

"Why would a writer make cliffhangers?" asked Dooley. "Isn't that what IKEA does?"

"Not clothes hangers, Dooley," I said. "Cliffhangers."

"What's a cliffhanger?"

"It's like the rose ceremony," said Harriet. "From *The Bachelor*? Our handsome bachelor is about to hand out his final rose of the night and suddenly they cut to commercial and you can't wait to see what happens next." She nodded seriously. "*That's* a cliffhanger."

Dooley stared at her, obviously not seeing the connection between cliffhangers, roses and *The Bachelor*. But when he opened his mouth to ask a follow-up question, Odelia said, "We're almost there, you guys. So you know what to do, right?"

"We know," I said. "We're going to talk to any animal we can find."

"Any animal?" asked Harriet in an undertone. "Not just cats?"

"Any animal," I confirmed.

"I'm not talking to dogs," Harriet said determinedly. "No, I mean it. I draw the line at dogs. Dogs are filthy, especially street dogs. Just looking at them makes my skin crawl."

"But what if that particular dog has some very important information to share?" I asked. "Odelia wants us to be her eyes and ears out there." Not to mention her nose and taste buds, apparently. "So put your petty anti-dog sentiments aside for a moment and think about the greater good here, Harriet."

"Yes, think about the greater good, Harriet," Dooley echoed.

"I mean, what if this particular mutt got a good look at

the killer's face? Are you going to let him get away just because you don't like dogs?"

"Are you, Harriet?" asked Dooley. "Are you going to let him get away?"

Harriet bridled at this. "You know what? If you like dogs so much why don't you talk to them? I'll stick to cats."

Dooley thought about this for a moment. "All right," he said finally. "I'll take the dogs—you take the cats." Then he directed a curious look at Brutus. "What species of animal are you going to talk to, Brutus?"

"I'll take the ladies," said Brutus with a big grin before he could stop himself. But when Harriet directed a withering look in his direction, he quickly added, "Or you could talk to the ladies, Harriet. I can talk to the gentlemen."

"We're here," said Odelia, and stomped on the brake with such fervor that the four of us were suddenly catapulted from our positions on the backseat and plastered against the back of the front seats. All of us except Dooley, who'd been sitting in the middle. He flew through the air, describing a perfect arc, and would have been reduced to a mere smear on the windshield if Odelia hadn't had the presence of mind—and the superior reflexes—to grab him by the neck and save him from further harm.

"Phew," said Dooley once he'd recovered from his adventure. "Thanks, Odelia."

"I'm sorry about that," said Odelia, giving Dooley a quick hug before placing him on the passenger seat. She turned to face us. "I know I'm a little on edge right now, but that's because my mom is in trouble. So please do the best you can, and I apologize for being such a sourpuss." She gave us a quick smile, then opened the door and allowed us to hop from the car and onto the pavement.

I saw she'd parked a ways away from the library. She probably didn't want to advertise the fact that she'd called in her private feline army to deal with this latest murder emergency. Even though Odelia can talk to cats, and so can her mother and grandmother, no one else can, and they would think it strange if they saw a grown woman speak feline.

We watched Odelia lock up her pickup and stalk away in the direction of the library. I felt for my human. She looked more stressed and downhearted than I'd ever seen her.

"I hope they don't lock up my human," said Harriet, who must have read my mind.

"They won't," I assured her. "Your human's brother is the chief of police, and he would never lock up his own sister. Humans don't lock up their own kin."

Actually, they probably did, but this wasn't the time to discuss worst-case scenarios. This was the time to rally round and tackle this dreadful murder business which had suddenly struck very close to home indeed.

"Let's do this," I said, and we were off to the races.

CHAPTER 4

*W*hen Odelia tried to enter the library she discovered a police officer had been stationed at the front door—possibly the first time that had ever happened. He was one of those stalwart types: buff, with a slight pudginess in the belly area, and sporting a nicely trimmed mustache, which doubled as a donut crumb collector.

"Um, I need to get in there?" she said tentatively.

She'd recognized the cop as one of her uncle's guys and she was pretty sure the cop had recognized her as well. He shook his head, though, and stared over her head as if silently hoping she would take a hint and simply melt away into the background.

"Oh, come on, Jackson," she said. "Don't give me that dead cod look."

This stirred him out of his self-chosen apathy. "I don't look like a dead cod," he said indignantly.

"Yes, you do. Now are you going to let me in? My mom is in there and she needs me."

"Your mom is a suspect, Poole, and unless you're her lawyer you're not setting foot anywhere near her."

"I was wrong," she said. "You're not a dead cod. You're dead, period. Or at least dead from the neck up." She tapped his noggin. "Yup. Just what I suspected. Solid ivory."

He had the good grace to look offended. "I'm just doing my duty. Please go away."

"I'm not going anywhere, but if you don't step aside you're the one who's going away."

That seemed to register. Officer Jackson obviously knew that Odelia was his boss's niece, and not just any old niece but the man's favorite niece, who'd helped him out with quite a few investigations in the recent past. What was more, she was now dating one of Hampton Cove's foremost police detectives.

He still continued undecided, though. That's the trouble with making decisions: either way you go, there are going to be consequences so it's probably better not to do anything.

Odelia decided to try a different tack. "Come on, Jackson. Have a heart. That's my mother in there. What if it were your mom?"

"My mom would never get involved with murder," he said a little huffily.

"Hey, that's something we've got in common: my mom wouldn't get involved with murder either!"

He rolled his eyes. "Chief Lip told me not to let anyone in so I'm not letting anyone in." Clearly feeling this was the last thing he was prepared to say on the matter, he clasped his hands behind his back and directed his gaze in the middle distance, studiously ignoring this pesky troublemaker.

Incensed, she poked him in the stomach, burying her index finger to the knuckle.

"Hey! That's police property," he sputtered, touching the offended spot.

"Oh, fine," she said, throwing up her hands and walking off. She turned back to the cop, walking backward now. "This isn't over, Jackson. You know that, right?"

"Yeah, yeah, yeah," he said, making a throwaway gesture.

She hurried around the side of the library, where a paved footpath was lined by mulch-covered patches of rosebushes, made her way to the back, then hung a sharp left before arriving at the service entrance which doubled as the library's emergency exit. To her surprise, her uncle hadn't stationed anyone at this door, and she blew right through and into the short corridor that led to a small cafeteria and a dressing room slash storeroom where authors and guests could get changed before stepping onto the stage for their readings.

Odelia took a quick peek inside the dressing room and held up her hand in greeting for Sarah Flunk, another one of her uncle's officers.

"There's no one guarding the backdoor," she said.

"On it," said Sarah with a nod.

"Have you seen my mom?"

Sarah gestured with her head. "Library. Your uncle is talking to her now."

Moving past a stack of unpacked boxes—newly acquired books yet to be cataloged, Odelia pushed through the door and into the library. She'd arrived at the left of the stage, and the first thing she saw was Abe Cornwall, the county coroner, leaning over what was unmistakably the late Chris Ackerman—the self-proclaimed world's bestselling writer.

She blinked, not expecting to come upon the dead man quite so suddenly.

Chris Ackerman was still seated in his chair, leaning precariously to his right, a large crimson spot on his white shirt, a pen of some kind sticking out of his neck.

Abe looked up when he sensed her presence. "Oh, hey,

Odelia. I liked that piece you did on Philomena, the blind groundhog. Has the rescue shelter found her a new home yet?"

"Um…"

"Oh, well. If they haven't, my wife wants to take the plunge. Francine is simply crazy about pets, and figures why not a groundhog this time? Why always cats and dogs, right?"

"Right," said Odelia, staring at the dead man as if transfixed. Even though she'd reported on crime plenty of times in her career as a reporter, and solved more murders than most journos, the sight of a dead person never failed to unnerve her to a great extent.

Abe, a scruffy-looking man with a pronounced paunch and gray hair that seemed to explode from his scalp in classic Einstein-style, returned his attention to the dead writer. "Such a pity, huh? Francine loves his books. Especially his Max Frost series. Read every single one of them. I'm more of a science fiction and fantasy reader myself. Give me a good Asimov or Ursula Le Guin any day over Chris Ackerman." He shrugged and produced a cheerful smile. "I guess my wife will have to find herself a new favorite writer."

"How did he die?" asked Odelia.

"Fountain pen to the jugular. Or, more accurately, the carotid artery. Very apt, I suppose. For a writer, I mean. Mind you, there are better ways to go."

"I'll bet there are," she murmured.

Abe tsk-tsked as he scrutinized the fountain pen.

"What is it?" asked Odelia.

"Looks like he was killed with his own pen, too. That's not very nice."

Odelia agreed that killing a writer with his own pen was not a nice thing to do, and left the coroner to continue his examination.

Stepping off the stage, she spotted her mother seated in

the kids' section of the library, along with Uncle Alec, while Chase was talking to Odelia's dad while taking copious notes. Odelia's grandmother, meanwhile, was seated in the PC nook, surfing the web.

Odelia made a beeline for the pirate ship where her mother and uncle were seated, and the moment Mom spotted her, she got up, stepped out of the ship, and they hugged.

"I'm so happy you're here," said Mom. "This is a nightmare."

CHAPTER 5

*S*o we were sleuthing again. And if I say sleuthing I mean looking for clues the Hallmark Movies & Mysteries Channel way. I have to confess I'd never liked the Hallmark Channel before. Over at Marge and Gran's house they watch that stuff all the time, and it hasn't done Dooley any favors. It's turned him into a sappy cat. Sappy as in overly mawkish, especially when it comes to Harriet, on whom he's had a crush since just about forever.

Harriet and Brutus had gone off to circle the block and talk to any animal they met—except for dogs—Harriet was sticking to her decision not to let any mutt so much as breathe on her flawless white fur—and Dooley and I watched them stalk off. Yes, detective work is a lot like being a Mormon missionary: it's all about you and your buddy, knocking on doors and spreading the word.

"Max?" said Dooley, even before we'd put one paw in front of the other.

"Uh-huh?" I said, searching around for our first potential eyewitness.

"Can I talk to you?"

27

"You are talking to me, Dooley."

"I watched the Discovery Channel last night."

Progress. It would appear that the Hallmark Channel was losing its dominant position in the Poole household.

"And? What did you learn?" I asked.

He suddenly shivered. "Nothing good," he intimated.

This didn't surprise me. Oftentimes people—or as in the case of Dooley pets—respond to being weaned off the Hallmark Channel by experiencing dizzy spells and bouts of insomnia. "It'll pass," I assured him as I looked up at the streetlamp we were standing under, and wondered how long it would be before the first dog trotted over to use it as a urinal.

"There was this documentary on about the end of the world as we know it," Dooley continued. His eyes had widened to their full dilation. "Max—it won't be long now before the entire country is either swallowed up by a gigantic tsunami of ocean waves, or the earth simply opens up underneath us, or Yellowstone finally erupts and kills us all!"

Oh, boy. Maybe it wasn't such a good idea to advise Dooley to stop watching the Hallmark Channel after all. "Look, Dooley—I'm sure you misunderstood. Nothing is going to drown us or crush us or—"

"Cover us in boiling lava!"

"—or that. Are you sure you were watching the Discovery Channel and not some fringe crackpot conspiracy show?"

"I don't think so. Gran was watching so I decided to join her. And let me tell you—I was terrified!"

"What did Gran say?"

"She fell asleep five minutes in."

Good self-preservation strategy. "I'm sure there's nothing to worry about. It's called alarmism and it's never done anyone any good. Just forget you ever saw that show."

"It wasn't a show—it was real! They showed diagrams."

"Never trust a diagram."

"They had real scientists! They had PhDs!"

"Sure, sure," I said, wondering how to steer the conversation away from natural disasters and the end of the world and back to our all-important murder investigation.

"It was very scary. I think we should talk to Odelia. We need to move countries."

"And go where?"

He looked at me earnestly. "New Zealand. Mark Zuckerberg bought a house there."

"Oh, well, if Mark Zuckerberg bought a house, we should probably all go there."

He heaved a sigh of relief. "I knew you'd agree. Now we need to convince Odelia."

Just like a child, Dooley is impervious to irony. Luckily, also like a child, Dooley's attention span is extremely limited. So I simply decided to change the subject.

"I say we enter the library first," I announced.

"To talk to Odelia about the volcano?"

"To check the crime scene."

"Crime scene?"

"The dead body. Haven't you noticed that almost every Hallmark Movies & Mysteries Channel detective stumbles over a dead body in the opening scene and takes it from there?"

Dooley was staring at me. "I don't like dead bodies, Max."

"I don't like dead bodies either, Dooley. But like it or not, we're detectives now, and detectives look at dead bodies." I spread my paws. "It's the only way to solve the mystery."

He looked pensive for a moment, and I could almost see the wheels and gears in his head turning and grinding away. Finally, he said, "Fine. Let's look at the dead body."

"I mean, how can we solve a crime if we don't know what the crime is all about?"

So we crossed the road and tripped up to the library. A large cop was blocking the door, so we decided to go around back, where hopefully there would be another way in.

To be perfectly honest I wasn't looking forward to visiting this so-called crime scene either, but if watching my fair share of Hallmark Movies & Mysteries had taught me one thing, it was that most detectives weren't born sleuths but had sleuthing thrust upon them.

All I ever wanted was to be a regular, happy-go-lucky cat, but through some strange twist of fate I'd had my human Odelia thrust upon me, and she had thrust detecting upon me and now here I was thrusting the same thing upon Dooley. Trying to figure out why one human murdered another human. I guess sometimes life is just weird that way.

CHAPTER 6

"*S*o what happened?"

Odelia's mom shook her head. "One minute he was fine, and the next he was... dead." She looked up, and Odelia didn't like the look of anguish on her mother's face. "Do you think he could have done this to himself? That I was talking to a man in great psychological pain, suffering through great stress, and that I didn't pick up the signs?"

"The coroner seems to think it was murder," said Odelia carefully.

"No one sticks a pen in their own neck, Marge," said Uncle Alec gruffly.

Odelia directed a censorious look at her uncle. He was a fine police officer, but his bedside manner left something to be desired. Uncle Alec, a rotund man with russet sideburns and an equally ruddy face, held up his hands in supplication and heaved his bulk out of the pirate ship. Since the ship wasn't made for humans—and definitely not for outsized humans—it took Alec some wriggling and silent cursing before he managed to exit the ship, hike up his pants and stalk off.

"I'll be over there—talking to my mother," he muttered.

"Oh, honey, you have to figure out what happened," said Mom the moment they were alone. She'd grasped Odelia's hands and squeezed them tightly. "A man was murdered. In my library. Who would do such a thing?"

It wasn't immediately clear whether she was talking about the murder or the fact that the killer had chosen the library as the place to do his or her dirty work, but Odelia decided to put her mother's mind at ease. "I'm on it, Mom." She darted a quick look around to see if Chase wasn't anywhere in the vicinity. "And so are the cats."

"You enlisted the cats? So quickly?"

"I picked them up before I drove down here. They're searching around for witnesses and clues as we speak."

Her mother didn't seem reassured by this evidence of feline sleuthing prowess. "Your uncle thinks this might be the work of a common thief. Chris Ackerman's wallet is gone, and so is his watch, his phone and whatever other valuables he might have had on his person."

"They probably came in through the service entrance while you weren't watching," said Odelia thoughtfully.

"I only let the man out of my sight for, like, half an hour or so! I was talking to Tex and your grandmother, checking the front of the library, when I heard a strange sound."

"What sound?"

"Like a cry? That must have been the moment he was attacked. Oh, my goodness. To think we were so close to the killer. If only I hadn't left Mr. Ackerman he might still be alive."

"Or you might be dead, too," said Odelia.

Her mother emitted a soft whimper. "What a horrible thing. And now people are going to say I did this—or your grandmother."

"I'm sure they won't."

But her mother wasn't listening. "At the very least they'll accuse me of gross negligence. I allowed the world's favorite writer to be murdered on my watch. At the library! Which is supposed to be a safe haven. A place where people come to be transported into another world."

Chris Ackerman definitely had been transported into another world. Permanently. Odelia watched as Chase stood chatting with the coroner—presumably trying to wrangle an initial report from the man.

"How was your date, by the way?" asked Mom, her sad demeanor suddenly replaced with a more cheerful expression. "Did Chase finally pop the question?"

"Mom!"

"What? You've been dating for so long now it's almost as if he doesn't *want* to marry you."

"Marriage is the furthest thing from our minds, Mom."

"Oh, that bad, huh? At least tell me he broke the news to you gently."

"What news?"

"That he's seeing another woman."

Odelia produced a frustrated noise at the back of her throat. "He's not seeing another woman, Mom. And why would he ask me out on a date to break up with me?"

"It's the proper way to end things. Go out on a high note."

"He was working his way towards something, but it wasn't a breakup."

"So what was it?" She clasped her hands to her mouth. "He's already married!"

"What? No! I think he was going to suggest we move in together, only you called and then Uncle Alec called and then we both had to leave."

"Oh, I'm so sorry, honey," said Mom. "If I'd known I wouldn't have called."

"What are you talking about? It's a good thing you did.

33

This has been a very traumatic experience for you, Mom."
She patted her mother's hand. "How is Gran taking it?"

Mom cocked an eyebrow in Gran's direction. "She's just
fine. I think she's even enjoying the whole thing. Something
to tell her friends. Or write about on her blog."

"Gran has a blog?"

"Blog or vlog. I'm not sure."

"I'll have a word with her."

"About the blog?"

"About the murder."

"Oh, right."

Apparently the trauma had already worn off. Poole
women were resilient, that much was obvious.

here was a policewoman guarding the back entrance but she was A) smoking, which meant the door was conveniently propped open, and B) intently studying her smartphone, which precluded her from seeing two cats sneak in right under her nose.

"I didn't like the sight of that, Max," said Dooley.

"Me, neither. I'm not a taxpayer but it's sad when cops are this negligent."

He gave me a look of confusion. "I meant the storm clouds, Max. Extreme weather is a precursor to the apocalypse. Do you think they'll allow us to enter New Zealand?"

"Why wouldn't they?"

"Johnny Depp's dogs weren't allowed to enter."

"Pretty sure that was Australia, not New Zealand, buddy."

"Phew," said Dooley.

We'd been prancing through a short corridor, and I was starting to wonder where we'd find the crime scene we were looking for. As the lead detective on this case it kinda bothered me that I hadn't been given sufficient information to locate the victim's body.

The door at the end of the corridor suddenly swung open and a large man with a potbelly appeared. When he caught sight of us, he halted in his tracks and squeezed his eyes shut for a moment, then actually started rubbing them. When he opened his eyes again Dooley and I were gone—having deftly scooted into a small room to our immediate left. I didn't know who this man was, but I was pretty sure I'd seen him before, so he was probably a cop, and wouldn't take kindly to civilians trampling all over his crime scene.

The room we found ourselves in contained several book-cases laden with boxes, a small table with two chairs, and a large framed picture of Marge, Tex, and Odelia. Smaller pictures had been placed underneath it, and one of them was a group picture of me, Dooley, Harriet and Brutus!

"Aw, look, Max," said Dooley. "Someone's taken our picture and put it up on that wall over there."

"Marge," I said. "She works at the library."

"She does? That explains things."

It certainly did. My gaze had traveled upwards and now rested on an empty pizza box that had been left on the table. There was also a briefcase, and when I jumped up on the table to take a closer look, I saw that it contained the initials CA. Chris Ackerman. When I realized that this briefcase had belonged to the dead man, I also realized that the potbellied policeman could enter this room any moment now to take a closer look at the briefcase, and I quickly jumped down from the table again.

Just at that moment, the door started to open.

"Dooley! Up there!" I hissed, and hurried over to the bookcase, then leaped on top of that and from there to the top of the concrete brick wall, which held a space where some species of metal ventilation tubes had been fed through into the next room.

Dooley, who was right behind me, sat panting for a moment.

"That was close," he whispered.

We both stared down at the man who'd entered the room. It was the same man we'd seen in the corridor. I now saw he was carrying a small briefcase of his own, which he placed on top of the table. He then studied Chris Ackerman's briefcase intently, meanwhile outfitting his hands with plastic gloves.

The door opened again and Chief Alec walked in. "And what have we here, Abe?"

"Briefcase, presumably belonging to the dead man," said Abe.

Alec flicked open the discarded pizza box, noticed it was empty, and flicked it closed again. "If this is a robbery gone wrong, wouldn't the perp have taken the briefcase?"

"That's your department, Alec. The only thing I'm interested in is finding out if there are any fingerprints on this thing that can help you nab the killer."

"It's so great to see how professionals handle an investigation, isn't it, Dooley?" I said. "And we have a front-row seat, too." When no response came, I repeated, "Dooley?"

Turning, I saw that I was talking to thin air. Dooley was gone.

"Psst! Max!" suddenly his voice called out to me.

I looked over my shoulder and saw he'd disappeared into the next room. I followed suit and soon discovered we were in the library itself, looking down on a small stage where a man was seated on a chair. Judging from the way he was slumped over, he seemed to be fast asleep. And that's when I saw it: something was sticking out of his neck!

"That's him!" I cried. "That's our dead guy!"

The discovery that we'd found what we were looking for didn't bring Dooley the jolt of joy I expected. Instead, he produced a loud yelp—not unlike the kind of squeaky sound Cameron Tucker of *Modern Family* fame tends to produce.

And then Dooley dropped off the wall, straight onto the dead body down below.

CHAPTER 8

*Y*ou know how they say cats always manage to land on all fours, right? Well, there's some truth to that. At least, for most cats. Dooley, unfortunately, managed to hit the dead man right on the noggin, bounced off him and then landed on the floor—on all fours.

It was pretty neat to watch, and if I'd had a smartphone, not to mention opposable thumbs, I would have caught it all on video, to post on my Instagram, where it would have gone viral and garnered millions of views in a matter of hours.

As it was, the only witness to Dooley's complicated acrobatics were me, myself and I. And as soon as I'd recovered from the shock of watching my friend tumble into the abyss, I applauded him heartily.

"Way to go, Dooley!" I cried, momentarily forgetting we were supposed to be here in a strictly undercover capacity.

Dooley would have taken a bow, if he hadn't been too busy sitting on his butt and shaking his head, looking both dazed and confused.

"What happened?" he finally asked.

"You decided to take a closer look at the dead man so you

jumped!" I said, searching around for a way to get to Dooley without taking the plunge myself.

I'm not much of an athlete I'm sorry to say, and even though Odelia has put me on several diets, I'm a cat of Rubenesque proportions or, as a smart cat once said, blessed with a low point of gravity. As a consequence the ten feet to the floor seemed... challenging.

"I think I hit the dead man, Max," said Dooley, still looking as if he'd been picked up and squashed down by the hand of God. "Do you think he'll mind?"

"He's dead so I'm pretty sure he won't."

"He doesn't look happy."

"That's because someone killed him. You wouldn't look happy if someone killed you."

At this point, I'd given up on navigating my way down to the floor and had decided to sit this one out. I had a great view of the victim and could do all the detecting from up there. And I'd just found a nice spot to sit and relax when all of a sudden this nice spot dropped out from underneath me. One moment it was there, and then it wasn't, if you see what I mean.

Moments later, I landed with my butt on the dead man's head, ricocheted away, and landed—on all fours—right next to Dooley.

I blinked a few times, wondering what was going on, when suddenly Dooley bellowed, "Timber!" and grabbed me by the shoulder, giving me a vigorous shove.

We managed to jump out of the way as the dead writer fell out of his chair and crashed to the floor. He bounced once, then lay immobile, a cloud of dust kicking up.

Dooley and I both coughed and stared at the dead man, who stared right back at us.

It was not a pleasant sight, nor was it the proudest moment in my career as a feline sleuth. Feline sleuths—or any sleuths for that matter—don't make a habit of thumping murder victims on the noggin—twice!—and knocking them out of their chairs. It's just not done. At least not to my knowledge—which now extended to at least one movie in all of the Hallmark Movies & Mysteries Channel franchises, including but not restricted to *Garage Sale Mysteries, Aurora Teagarden Mysteries, Fixer Upper Mysteries* and *Hailey Dean Mysteries*.

Before we could respond, though, we were surrounded. Surrounded by humans. Lucky for us they were all humans we were familiar with: Odelia, Marge, Tex, Uncle Alec, Gran, and even Odelia's solid cop boyfriend, Chase Kingsley.

"What do we have here?" asked Alec with a frown. "Two cats and a dead man."

"Add a parrot and you have all the makings of a pretty funny joke," Tex quipped and laughed loudly at his own joke. When no one else laughed, he quickly cut the laughter short.

"I'm so sorry," I said. "We slipped and fell."

It was a terribly embarrassing thing to say. I don't normally slip and fall. Then again, I'm only feline, after all. These things happen to the best of cats, right?

"What's that?" asked Odelia suddenly, pointing at something on the floor.

It was a cream-colored envelope, with a logo embossed on the front.

"Don't touch it," said Uncle Alec when Marge made a move to pick it up. "Abe!" he bellowed. "Come in here a second, will ya?!"

Abe came running. "What, what, what?" the voluminous man asked, panting.

Uncle Alec pointed down at the envelope and Abe frowned. "Huh. Where did that come from? And why have you moved the body without my explicit permission?"

There was a slight pause, then Gran said, "He fell."

"He fell?"

"He fell," Gran repeated. "Keeled over. It happens."

Abe didn't look convinced. With the air of a man who'd done that kind of thing a thousand times before, he pulled on a fresh pair of gloves, bent down with some effort, and picked up the envelope, then turned it over in his hands. "Buckerfield Publishing."

"That's Chris Ackerman's publisher," said Marge, who knew her way around books—being a librarian and all. "Or at least it was his publisher. I read somewhere that he recently signed a ten-book deal with Franklin Cooper, rumored to have netted him a neat sum."

"Well, open it," said Gran.

Abe cleared his throat officiously, then opened the envelope and extracted a sheet of paper. Like the envelope, it was beige and embossed with the same logo. He quickly scanned the document's contents and frowned. "Signed Malcolm Buckerfield. Says here he's making Ackerman a counteroffer. Practically begs him not to change publishers. Offers him…" Abe gulped a little, like a turkey about to gobble up a particularly tasty morsel. "Holy mackerel."

"Just spit it out, Abe," said Uncle Alec.

Abe's eyes rose over the document to meet Alec's. "Ten million smackeroos if you please."

"Nice," croaked Gran. "This Chuck Peckerwood was some rich dude." She directed a reverent look at the dead man. "Too bad he's dead. We might have hit it off."

"Instead, someone hit *him* off," Uncle Alec grunted.

Abe suddenly fixed his eyes on me. "What the hell is that cat doing in here?"

CHAPTER 9

*H*arriet and Brutus were reluctantly wandering the streets around the library. They were nice streets, on the whole, featuring nice houses, but they lacked a certain oomph. The kind of oomph Harriet got from watching *The Bachelor*, for instance, or *The Kardashians*. To be honest she was more of a homebody. Perched on her throne —a nice comfy red velvet cushion—in the Poole living room, grooming herself and watching her favorite reality shows, she was in her element. Roaming these streets at night talking to random cats? Not!

"I don't like this, Brutus," she said now. "Let's go home."

"But we haven't talked to a single cat."

"And we won't. Isn't it obvious they're all home? Doing what we should be doing?"

"Nookie?"

She giggled. "Watching *The Bachelor*, you big doofus. With nookie for dessert."

Brutus didn't respond. He wasn't as big on *The Bachelor* as Harriet and Gran were. He probably liked *The Bachelorette* a lot more, even though with Brutus it was hard to be sure.

Lately he'd been in one of his silent moods. Not talking much. Harriet hated it.

"Why don't we leave the sleuthing to Max and Dooley," she tried again. "This is more Max's thing anyway. He's the one who wants to become a super sleuth. He's the one who's so obsessed with these silly Hallmark shows, figuring they'll teach him everything he needs to know."

"Well, he's got a point," said Brutus. "They are some pretty neat shows."

Harriet scowled at her mate. "Neat? What's so neat about people looking for clues the whole time?"

"They're solving murders. Someone should," said Brutus vaguely.

"The police should. That's what they're paid to do. Like your human Chase. The rest of us? We should simply live our lives, oblivious and happy."

Brutus cocked an eyebrow. "Don't let Max hear you say that. He wants to contribute."

"Max is misguided. And so is Dooley. It's all Odelia's fault, really. She should never have gotten us involved in all of her amateur sleuthing. I mean, she's a reporter, for crying out loud. When did reporters get it into their heads that they should be crime fighters?"

"I guess it kinda goes with the territory?" said Brutus.

"No, it doesn't." Harriet had given this matter a great deal of thought. "Besides, it's dangerous. Criminals don't like it when people mess with their livelihoods. Odelia should leave well enough alone, and so should Max. Before you know it one of those murderers or whatever decides to strike back and then where does that leave us? Without a human."

This seemed to give Brutus pause, just like Harriet had known it would. "Do you think one of these murderers might target Odelia?"

"Of course! What does a murderer do? He murders. Like

a plumber unclogs pipes or a coin collector collects coins, a murderer murders. It's what they do. So if you're going to try and stop them, they're bound to get upset and murder you before you know it."

Brutus pondered this. "Mh," he said. "Something in that."

"Of course there's something in that. If there's one thing you should know about me by now, Brutus, it's that I'm always right."

Brutus didn't seem convinced, and soon lapsed into silence once more. It irked Harriet a great deal. She didn't mind a silent mate—she talked enough for two—but she had the impression he wasn't consistently paying attention, and that, she simply couldn't stand.

A scrawny cat with matted fur crossed the road in front of them, stared for a moment, then scrambled off.

"Shouldn't we talk to him?" Brutus asked. "Ask him what he saw?"

Harriet rolled her eyes. "Who cares what he saw or didn't see?"

Brutus gave her a hesitant look, then cleared his throat. "Buddy—hey, buddy!"

"Brutus!" hissed Harriet. "What do you think you're doing?"

But Brutus was already jogging in the direction of the scrawny cat.

"Whaddya want?" the cat asked suspiciously.

"I don't know if you know," said Brutus, "but there's been a murder at the library."

"Is that right?" said the cat, not the least bit impressed.

"Yeah, a writer was murdered. So I was wondering if maybe you saw something?"

The cat eyed Brutus with a look of amusement. "Like what?"

"Like maybe you saw the killer or something?"

The cat laughed. "What are you? A cat sleuth?"

Brutus shrugged. "Yeah, I guess you could say that."

"Oh, boy. Of all the weird stuff…" The cat studied Harriet, who sat studiously ignoring both the raggedy cat and Brutus. "So who's the dame?"

"That's Harriet."

"So is she also a cat sleuth?"

Brutus hesitated. "Um…"

The cat laughed again. "Gotcha." He raised his voice. "Hey, toots! Over here!"

Harriet felt heat rise to her cheeks and her tail quiver. "Are you talking to me?"

"Yeah, I'm talking to you. You wanna know what I saw, I can tell you for a price."

Harriet rolled her eyes again, a gesture she'd perfected. "Oh, my God."

"Ralph, not God."

"What?"

"My name is Ralph, not God. Now how about you show me some affection and I show you—hey! What's the big idea?!"

In a lightning-fast move, Brutus had unsheathed the razor-sharp claws of his right front paw and had raked them across the scruffy cat's visage. The transformation from benign wannabe cat sleuth to savage vigilante had been swift and frankly damn impressive.

"Don't you dare talk to my girlfriend like that," Brutus snarled.

His tail was distended, his back arched, and there was a cold, menacing look in his eyes that told anyone who watched that here was a cat who was not gonna be messed with.

"All right, all right!" cried the scrawny cat, licking a drop of blood from his face. "No need to go all Hannibal Lecter on me, big fella!" He started to walk away but stopped when Brutus produced a growling sound at the back of his throat. The small cat gulped.

"Tell me what you saw," Brutus growled.

"I saw nothing, all right!" cried the cat, recoiling.

"You said you saw something."

"I was just messing with you! I know nuthin!"

And with these words, the cat tucked his tail between his legs and scooted off.

"Dang it," Brutus rasped in a guttural voice that was as impressive as his physique.

"Dang it is right," Harriet purred as she traipsed up. "Why, Brutus, that was amazing."

Brutus was still staring after the cat, a dark gleam in his eye. "I should go after him."

"Oh, don't bother. You heard what he said. He didn't see a thing." She gave Brutus a loving nudge. "The way you defended me, Brutus. Oh, my. I have goosebumps all over."

Brutus gave her a sad look. "Maybe you're right. Maybe I'm not cut out for this."

This surprised Harriet. "I never said that. I merely tried to point out that—"

"Let's go home," said Brutus. He suddenly looked deflated. And as he stalked off, Harriet couldn't shake the feeling that there was something wrong with her mate.

"Brutus!" she yelled as she tripped after him. "We could ask some more cats if you want—maybe even dogs and vermin. Seeing as we came all the way out here and all."

But Brutus seemed to have lost his taste for sleuthing. "I just wanna go home," he muttered, and then he sauntered off, his head low, all the fight having left him.

CHAPTER 10

*I*t had finally happened. For perhaps the first time in our lives our very own humans had escorted us from a building. Odelia, Marge and Grandma, in a concerted effort, had picked us up and kicked us out of the library.

"I can't believe they would do such a thing!" I cried.

"They were very nice about it," Dooley commented.

He didn't seem to mind one bit. But I did.

"Nice or not, I hate it when they treat us like animals."

"We are animals," Dooley reminded me.

"Yes, but they treated us like pets!"

"We are pets."

"Yes, I give you that, but to kick us out like that!"

"They did it in the nicest possible way, though."

He was right. They had. Odelia had whispered into my ear that she was very sorry but that this Abe Cornwall guy was a very important person at the county coroner's office and if she allowed us to stick around he might kick up a fuss which would land Uncle Alec in hot water with the powers that be. What those powers were, she didn't say. Powers that be? Be what? Marge had added her two cents by pecking kisses on my head and Dooley's and even Gran had been very sweet and given us tickles and cuddles before chucking us out.

"I don't like this, Max," said Dooley suddenly. "I don't like this one bit."

"I'm glad you finally agree." But then I saw he was darting anxious glances at the sky again. "Oh, not again with the apocalypse, Dooley. I'm telling you, the world isn't ending."

"Yes, it is. All scientists agree. And scientists know their stuff. That's why they're scientists."

It was one of those spurious arguments that are hard to contradict so I decided not to bother. At some point Dooley would realize that the world wasn't ending and forget all about it. At least I hoped that he would. I really didn't need this apocalypse nonsense.

We were pacing up and down the street that backed the library. Before she'd poured me from her arms, Odelia had said, "The killer most likely came in through the service entrance, so if you could find a witness, it could help me crack this case."

Cracking cases is what I did for a living, so we'd been hanging around that back entrance hoping to catch sight of one of those illustrious witnesses ever since.

"What's a witness, Max?" Dooley finally asked. "And how do we find one?"

"A witness is someone who's seen something that's important," I said.

"Like what?"

"Like the killer going in through that back entrance, murder weapon in hand. A good witness is someone who remembers what the killer looked like, what he was wearing, what color his hair was and all that good stuff. The stuff a detective can use to identify a culprit."

"How do you know so much about this, Max?" said

Dooley, and I won't conceal his words were the ego-boost I needed after being removed from the scene of the crime.

"I'll tell you exactly how I know so much about it, Dooley. It's because I—"

"What are you two morons doing here?" suddenly a voice rudely interrupted me.

We both looked up and saw that none other than Clarice was addressing us from the top of the nearest dumpster.

"Clarice!" cried Dooley. "It's so great to see you!"

It was hard to determine whether the feeling was mutual. If I had to hazard a guess, I'd say it wasn't. Her next words confirmed this.

"If you're here to steal my food I can tell you right now I will beat you and I will kick you and when I'm done beating and kicking you I will scratch you and then I will bite you."

Yep. That's Clarice in a nutshell: a no-nonsense feral cat who'd just as soon cut you to ribbons than give you a hug. Life on these Hampton Cove mean streets will teach you that. Or at least that's what she keeps telling us.

"We're not here to steal your food," I assured her.

"You're looking great, Clarice," said Dooley with a grin.

She had a fresh scratch across her nose, and her mottled red hide featured more bald spots than the last time I'd seen her, but she did look slightly fuller. Then again, I knew for a fact that Odelia left food out for her from time to time, so she didn't really have to dumpster-dive for a living if she didn't want to. I guess she wanted to. Or maybe it had become a force of habit.

"You look terrible," growled Clarice. "And so do you, Max. You're fat. How much do you weigh these days? A hundred pounds?"

"I'll have you know that twenty pounds is the new ten pounds," I said haughtily.

"Max isn't fat," said Dooley. "He's a cat of substance. Isn't that right, Max?"

"Exactly right."

"You didn't answer my question," said Clarice. "What are you morons doing here?"

"We're looking for clues," said Dooley.

"Witnesses," I corrected him. "We looked for clues before."

"And we found one," said Dooley. "He was dead and had a pen sticking out of him."

"That wasn't a clue—that was the victim," I said. "Terminology is everything, Dooley."

"So are you a witness, Clarice?" asked Dooley.

"A witness to what?" she growled, casually licking her paw.

"A man was murdered inside the library tonight," I explained. "A famous thriller writer called Chris Ackerman. The killer most likely snuck in through the back entrance. So now we're trying to locate anyone who might have seen this killer—an eyewitness."

"What do you care that humans get killed?" asked Clarice with a frown.

Clarice had a grudge against humans. Ever since her own human dumped her in the forest on the outskirts of town, she hasn't forgiven him—or the entire species he belonged to. Though to be honest, what human would dump a beloved pet? A human like that probably doesn't even deserve to be called human. Unhuman, maybe? Or inhuman?

"Odelia asked us to investigate," I explained. "And when Odelia asks us to do something, it's a privilege and a pleasure for us to comply."

"We love our human," said Dooley fervently. "We'd do anything for her."

Clarice was shaking her head. "So dumb," she muttered, and hopped down from the dumpster. And as she started stalking off, she turned and said, "Ask Big Mac. I saw him skulking around here earlier this evening. Chances are he saw something."

"Big Mac?" I asked. "Who's Big Mac?"

"Big fat cat like you," she said. "You'll like him. It's like looking into a mirror."

"Where do we find this Big Mac?" I asked, deciding not to be triggered by this slur.

"McDonald's. Where else?" And then she was gone, swallowed up by the darkness.

We sat staring after her for a moment. I could feel chills running down my spine.

"She just disappeared, Max," said Dooley reverently. "How does she do that? Do you think she's a ghost?"

"She's something, all right."

"I'm just glad she's on our side."

I wasn't absolutely sure she was on our side. With Clarice you just never know.

"At least she gave us a very important clue," said Dooley.

"A witness," I corrected him.

"A clue to a witness," he said, and he wasn't wrong this time.

ncle Alec put down his phone. He was looking grim.

"Chase. Better come along," he snapped. "They found him."

"Found who?" asked Odelia.

"The killer." He turned to Odelia's mom. "With any luck this'll all be over tonight, honey."

"That would be great," said Mom.

"Can I tag along?" asked Odelia as her uncle and Chase made for the door.

"Sure. Why not?" said the Chief. "You better go home," he added for Mom, Tex and Gran's sake. "No sense in sticking around here."

"But I have to close the library," said Mom. "I can't just leave it open all night."

"My people will close up shop, Marge," said Uncle Alec with a smile. "You go on home and try to get some sleep. You, too, Ma. Can you make sure they get home safe, Tex?"

"Will do," Odelia's dad confirmed.

"I'm gonna tag along with you, Alec," said Gran.

All eyes turned to the old lady.

"What? Odelia can come and I can't? This is ageism pure and simple."

Uncle Alec grimaced. "This is police business, Ma. Nothing to do with you."

"Everything's to do with me," she countered. "I'm a detective in my own right, and I want to see this man's killer brought to justice." She vaguely gestured in the direction of the stage, where Chris Ackerman's body had already been removed by Abe Cornwall's crew.

"Mom, you're not a detective," said Marge quietly.

"But I want to be." She directed a cheerful look in Odelia's direction. "Teach me?"

Odelia opened her mouth, then closed it again. Whatever she'd been expecting, it wasn't this. "But-but-but..." she sputtered.

"That's settled then," said her grandmother, and hooked arms with her. "Let's crack this case wide open, darlin'. And show those bad 'uns what Poole women are made of."

Dad made a strangled noise at the back of his throat, Mom looked stunned, Uncle Alec was rubbing his sideburns as if hoping to produce a genie that would spirit Grandma away for good, and Chase was trying not to laugh. All in all, Gran had probably produced the effect she'd been aiming for. Odelia thought her grandmother would have made a great actress. One of those divas of old, like Elizabeth Taylor or Bette Davis. She certainly knew how to hold an audience spellbound with her antics and her harebrained schemes.

They made for the exit, and as they walked out, Odelia nodded a kindly greeting at the officer guarding the door. "Hey, Jackson. Still hanging around, I see?"

Jackson went a little goggle-eyed. "How did you get in?"

"Magic," said Odelia, doing the jazz hands thing.

"Don't just stand there, Jackson," Uncle Alec grumbled. "Make yourself useful."

"Yes, sir," said Officer Jackson, practically jumping to attention. He considered his superior officer's words. "What do you want me to do, sir?"

Uncle Alec fixed him with a stern look. "Write up your report. I want it on my desk first thing in the morning. And make sure to leave nothing out."

"Yes, sir," said Jackson happily. Typing up reports appeared to be his strong suit.

As they proceeded down the few steps that led to the library's courtyard, Uncle Alec grunted, "Told you you couldn't go in, eh?"

"Yeah, he said you told him not to let anyone in so that's what he did. You can't blame him, really. He's one of those people who refuse to think for themselves."

"He's an idiot," Alec grumbled. "So how did you get in?"

"Back entrance. The same way the killer got in."

Uncle Alec darted a quick look around, but Chase had already crossed the street, where he'd parked his car, and Mom and Dad and Gran stood arguing nearby. "What did your cats find out?" Alec asked, arching an inquisitive eyebrow and lowering his voice.

"So far nothing. Except for the letter from Ackerman's publisher."

"Mh. Abe would have found that eventually, but you're right. Nice work."

Odelia didn't mention that Max and Dooley finding that letter had been a side-effect from falling on Chris Ackerman's head. Sometimes accidents do happen, and in this case they'd produced a new lead.

She headed for her car, and as she got in, found herself facing her grandmother, who was sitting in the passenger seat, hands folded on top of her purse. "You should lock your car," Gran said. "It's a small miracle no one stole it."

"It's just an old jalopy. No one in their right mind would steal it. What are you doing here? I thought Uncle Alec told you to go home and get some sleep?"

"And I told that old fool that I was coming with you." She pursed her lips. "You've got yourself a pardner, pardner. So put this car in gear and let's catch ourselves a killer."

Odelia shook her head as she jammed the key into the ignition. "From what I can gather the killer has been caught already. And he's being processed as we speak."

Gran didn't look convinced. "If I know Alec he probably caught the wrong 'un. So it's up to us to catch the right 'un. So step on it. Time's a-wastin' and the real killer is escapin.'"

Odelia clenched her jaw and started the car with a roar.

Oh, boy. This was going to be a barrel of laughs.

CHAPTER 12

delia and Gran stared through the one-way mirror while Uncle Alec and Chase interviewed the suspect who had just been arrested. Judging from his tattered clothes, his full red beard, and disheveled appearance, he was either a homeless man or a hipster.

"He doesn't look like a killer," Gran commented.

"What does a killer look like?" asked Odelia.

"It's all in the eyes," said Gran, gesturing at her own eyes. "A real killer has that dead, cold killer look. Looking into the eyes of a killer is like looking into the abyss. A cold abyss."

Was there any other kind of abyss? "So have you looked into a killer's eyes?"

"Oh, plenty of times. Leo was a killer, and I locked eyes with that man many times."

"Leo Wetland? Your ex-boyfriend?"

"He was never my boyfriend," snapped Gran. "We were lovers."

Odelia decided not to ask what the difference was. "I didn't know Leo was a killer."

"Oh, sure. Leo was big on killin'. He once took out a wasp

nest in his attic. Didn't bat an eye. Cold-hearted killer." She gestured at her eyes again. "Like looking into the—"

"Abyss. I get it."

"Look, I didn't do it, all right?!" the homeless guy—or hipster—exclaimed.

"That's what they all say," growled Gran.

"So what was Chris Ackerman's wallet doing in your pocket?" asked Uncle Alec.

"Yeah, okay, so I stole it. Sometimes I steal stuff. It's a disease. I'm seeing a doctor about it but so far the therapy isn't working. We're still fine-tuning. You can ask Dr. Freggar. He'll tell you all about it."

"Wait. Let me get this straight. You're telling us you stole Mr. Ackerman's wallet but you didn't kill him," said Uncle Alec.

"That's exactly what I'm telling you—and please note for the record that my disease compels me to steal stuff. It's not like I'm a thief or anything. It's a sickness. Like, um—like cancer. Or boils."

"Boils," grunted Uncle Alec.

"Yeah," grinned the man.

"We found Mr. Ackerman's wallet on you," said Chase, "as well as his diamond watch, a monogrammed money clip containing no less than five hundred dollars, a monogrammed money pouch with fifty bucks in loose change, and a monogrammed gilded iPhone also belonging to Mr. Ackerman and you're telling me you had nothing to do with his murder."

"He was dead when I found him!" cried the man, spreading his arms.

Uncle Alec pounded the table with his fist. "You're lying, Mr. Drood."

"Sasha," said the man. When Alec stared at him, he added with a genial smile, "My friends call me Sasha."

"You decided to rob Mr. Ackerman but he caught you. You struggled and you killed him," said Chase. "That's the truth, isn't it, Mr. Drood?"

"In an alternate reality maybe it is," said Sasha, settling back in his chair. "But in this reality I read somewhere that Chris Ackerman, the world's bestselling writer, was coming to Hampton Cove. Oh, I said to myself, the world's best-selling writer, I said. That probably means he's rich, I said. And if he's rich, he won't mind donating some of his money to a deserving sick person like myself. So I head on down to the library to have a conversation with Mr. Ackerman about his donation—only when I get there he's sitting all by his lonesome on stage. Dead as a dodo! So my *disease* tells me that since he's dead already he's not going to miss his pocket junk so I took it." He shrugged. "There's no law against that, is there?"

"Oh, this guy is good," Gran muttered. "Maybe I should get in there and slap him around some. Practice a little police brutality."

"You're not going in there, Gran," said Odelia. "Uncle Alec and Chase have got this."

"Why didn't you take his briefcase while you were at it?" asked Uncle Alec.

"Briefcase? He had a briefcase?"

"Yes, he did. So why didn't you take it?"

Sasha Drood tsk-tsked for a moment. "Dang it. I must have missed that." He held up a finger. "I mean, my *disease* must have missed that."

"The fountain pen you stabbed Mr. Ackerman with," said Chase, "is worth three thousand bucks. Why didn't you take that?"

"I told you guys already, I didn't stab—hold on, three thousand bucks?"

"At least."

"You're joshing me, right?" He darted amused glances at the two cops. "Now you're just yanking my chain. No pen is worth three thousand bucks."

"This one is. A genuine Graf von Faber-Castell fountain pen. Eighteen-carat gold nib."

Sasha was laughing out loud now. "You guys!" he cried. "And they say cops don't have a sense of humor!"

Chase and Alec were staring at the crook, not a flicker of a smile on their faces.

"Let me get in there," Gran said. "I'll teach this punk a lesson."

But Uncle Alec proved he was up to the task by slamming the table once again. "Just tell us the truth, Drood!" he snarled. "You killed Ackerman and you robbed a dead man!"

Sasha's laughter died away, as if turned off at the tap. He eyed Alec seriously. "Do you really think I'd leave a three-thousand-dollar fountain pen behind? You're crazy, Chief. No, I didn't kill that man. I only robbed him—correction, my *disease* robbed him. And if you don't believe me, Dr. Freggar will confirm everything I've just said. I have his number in my phone, in case you're interested."

Alec stared at the man. "Boils, huh?" he said.

Sasha Drood smiled widely. "Boils," he confirmed.

"You know? He doesn't look like a killer," said Odelia.

"Oh, but he does," said Gran. "Just look at his eyes. Dark pools of evil. I stared into eyes like that once, and I've never forgotten it."

"Leo?"

"Your dad when I told him I was moving back in." She smiled at the memory.

CHAPTER 13

"We must really love our human," said Dooley, slightly huffing and puffing.

We'd been walking for a while now, as there's only one McDonald's in town, and it's located in a strip mall on the main road into town, a little ways away from the library, which is in the heart of town.

"Why is that?" I asked, also puffing.

"Look at us walking a marathon! Just to please Odelia."

"You don't walk a marathon, Dooley. You run a marathon." But I got what he was saying. Clarice would have made fun of us if she'd seen us. Then again, we hadn't lied. Odelia was good to us, and so were Marge and Gran. Even the men in the family weren't too bad. Uncle Alec and Tex and Chase had installed a cat flap not so long ago. It had taken them several attempts before I managed to pass through without getting stuck but they'd done it. So it was understandable we should return the favor by being the best sleuths we could be.

Cars zoomed past us, and I couldn't help but wonder where they were all going. It was way past human bedtime, after all, and the only creatures who should be stirring were us cats. And maybe owls. And bats. And mice. Oh, and coyotes, of course. Just then, a loud howl rose up from the bushes nearby, and Dooley and I put a bit more pep in our step.

The first coyote had yet to be spotted on Long Island but you never knew. And I certainly didn't want to be the first one to spot it and be eaten by the darn thing!

Soon the strip mall's bright neon lights beckoned us and we headed straight for the McDonald's restaurant which, much to our surprise, was still open for business!

"Let's hope we find this Big Mac," I said as we headed straight for the dumpster parked on the McDonald's parking lot.

"I could use a Big Mac right now," lamented Dooley. "I'm starving."

"I'm pretty peckish myself," I admitted.

We'd been at this detecting business for hours now, and I could use some food. But duty called, and it wasn't as if I was going to starve to death by skipping a meal. Or two.

The McDonald's dumpster appeared pretty much deserted when we arrived, and my heart sank. Had we really come all this way for nothing? That was just sad. And a testament to the learning curve we were on as junior feline sleuths. This wouldn't have happened to Aurora Teagarden. When Aurora Teagarden went someplace she always found fresh clues. Or maybe the people making those Hallmark movies simply cut out all the boring parts.

"I think I hear something," said Dooley as we approached.

"A rat probably," I said, trepidation making me halt in my tracks. There are cats that eat rats. And then there's me and Dooley. We don't like rats. In fact rats scare me to death. They're big, they're mean, and they have some really sharp teeth. You get the picture.

"Who goes there?" suddenly a voice rose up from the dumpster's innards.

"It's a rat!" Dooley hissed. "Every cat for himself!" And he scooted off to hide underneath a parked Toyota Land Cruiser!

Suddenly a head appeared over the dumpster's edge. I stared at the head. The head stared back at me. Clarice had been right. It was like looking in a mirror. The head belonged to a blorange cat with a gorgeous set of whiskers and a pink-colored little button of a nose.

"Hey, Big Mac," I said, giving the cat a little wave.

"Hey, you," he said, then blinked confusedly. He picked up a piece of burger and stared at it, then back at me. "Some joker put shrooms in my burger. I'm hallucinating."

"No, you're not. I'm really here," I said. "My name is Max, and this…" I searched around for Dooley. "Um… Anyway. I'm here because Clarice sent me. You know Clarice, right?"

The big cat shivered visibly. "I wish I didn't. She scares me."

"She scares me, too."

Big Mac jumped down from the dumpster without dropping the piece of burger, which made him a superhero in my book. He studied me intently for a few moments, while I studied him. He was a little pudgier, but otherwise he could have been my brother from another mother. Or maybe even from the same mother. I'm not big on genealogy, so I never bothered to create my family tree, but now might be a good time to correct the oversight.

"Was your mom—" I began.

"Was your mom—" he simultaneously said.

We both grinned awkwardly.

"Were you born—" I said.

"Were you born—" he said.

From behind us, suddenly Dooley's voice rang out. "Oh. My. God. You guys look *exactly* the same!"

"Well, I'm a little slimmer," I said.

"You look really fit," said Big Mac. "Have you been working out?"

"Nah, not really," I said. "I just try to watch what I eat."

"He doesn't," said Dooley. "Odelia puts him on a diet from time to time, though."

"Odelia? Is that your human?" asked Big Mac.

I nodded. "She's great."

"How long have you had her?"

"Straight from the litter," I said.

"I don't actually remember my mother," said Big Mac, taking a tentative bite from the burger, then munching with enthusiasm when he failed to detect the taste of shrooms. "I mean, I know I had a mother, but my first memories are a little hazy. I remember I was with this old lady, but then she died, and I got transferred to her daughter, who didn't like cats, and then she passed me on to her cousin, who liked cats so much she kept a dozen, which was pretty horrible."

I nodded. Most cats hate other cats. Dooley and I are the exceptions to the rule, I guess. We genuinely like each other, and most other cats we meet. We're weird that way.

Big Mac heaved a deep sigh as he delved deep into his recollection. "Lemme see, what happened next—Oh, that's right. She got arrested for growing weed." He spread his paws. "And that's how I ended up here."

"On the street," I said, nodding. "Living from crumbs and scraps."

He frowned. "Are you kidding? My human runs this McDonald's. Feeds me all the burgers I want. He's the weed woman's brother and promised to look after us as long as his sister enjoys the hospitality of the Suffolk County penal system. Only problem is that since I live with him I've gained ten pounds. By the time Sissy gets released she won't recognize me." He devoured the final remnants of the burger and burped. "So what did Clarice want?"

"I don't get it," said Dooley. "If this man feeds you all the food you want, why are you—"

"Checking out this dumpster?" He shrugged. "Variety. You wouldn't believe what people throw away. Once I found a container of perfectly good chicken nuggets in here."

"But if you want chicken nuggets, why don't you ask your human?" said Dooley.

Big Mac stared at him, then laughed. "Ask my human! As if he could understand a word I say! You're funny, little guy."

I decided not to mention that our human could understand us perfectly. It would probably boggle his mind. Not to mention he might think we were yanking his chain.

"Clarice actually sent us here because she thought you might be a witness to a murder," I said, deciding to dispense with the chitchat and get down to brass tacks.

Big Mac's eyes went wide as… Big Macs. "Murder!"

"Over at the Hampton Cove library. Were you by any chance hanging out there?"

"I was," he said. "But I didn't see no murder. Not a one."

"It happened inside the library. Around eight o'clock-ish. Did you see anyone go in through the back entrance around that time?"

Big Mac thought hard, even sinking down on his haunches and puckering up his face. "Yeah," he said finally. "In fact I saw several people go in. I didn't pay them a lot of attention. Except for the pizza guy. I love pizza." He licked his lips. "The one thing McDonald's doesn't have. Which is the reason I like to head into town of an evening. There's a crazy tasty pizza joint right around the corner from the library. In fact there are two."

"Could you... identify these people?" I asked. "I mean, if you saw them again, would you recognize them?"

"Sure. Why? Do you think one of them was a killer?"

I nodded, an idea forming in my head. "What do you say we take you downtown to look at some pictures? And when you're through our human will buy you the biggest, juiciest, most delicious pizza you can imagine."

He licked his lips. "You've got to be kidding, right?"

"No, I'm not kidding," I said.

"He's not kidding," Dooley confirmed.

"Any pizza I want?"

"Any pizza you want."

"Oh boy, oh boy, oh boy," he said, rubbing his tummy. "You really are my brother, aren't you? And if you're not, you must be Santa Claus and Christmas came early this year!"

CHAPTER 14

*O*delia was convening with her uncle and Chase in Alec's office. This was business as usual for them. The only difference was that this time Gran had joined them and was now lecturing her son on how to do his job.

"Didn't I tell you to go home, Ma?" asked Uncle Alec wearily, rubbing his eyes with the palms of his hands.

"You can't keep a good sleuth down," Gran insisted with a wink in Odelia's direction.

"Oh, boy," Chase muttered, earning himself a scowl from the old lady.

"I think he did it," she said. "He's got that guilty look."

"I hate to agree with you, but I think for once you're right," said the Chief.

"For once? I'm always right," said Gran.

Alec ignored her. "This guy has a rap sheet as long as my arm. He's been arrested for stealing so many times it's a miracle he's still walking around a free man."

"It's a disease," said Chase with a lopsided grin. "And as we all know prison doesn't cure a man, only the attention of a fine medical man like Dr. Freggar does."

"He probably made that up," said Odelia. "I'll bet this Dr. Freggar doesn't exist."

"Oh, he exists," said Alec. "But that doesn't mean our Mr. Drood isn't a thief."

"But is he also a murderer," said Chase, rubbing his chin. "That's the question."

"I told you already," said Gran. "He's our guy! He did it! Now fry him in the chair!"

"It doesn't work like that, Ma," said Uncle Alec. "We just collect the evidence and collar the guy, then it's up to the DA to decide if they're going to prosecute or let him walk."

"At the very least he'll be charged with grand larceny," said Chase.

"Let's not get ahead of ourselves here," said Alec. "I think we have a pretty good case that Sasha Drood is our killer and that's what I'll tell the prosecutor in the morning." He yawned cavernously. "And now I'd like to go home and get some sleep myself."

"I think we can all use some sleep," said Odelia, also yawning.

She glanced up and saw that Gran was still sitting, ramrod straight, staring at Uncle Alec, not a sign of tiredness on her lined face. Even her curly perm was still perfectly in place, not a white curl ruffled. "So when are you going to string him up?" she asked.

"Ma! We don't string people up! This isn't the Old West. People have rights."

"This is a dangerous criminal we're talking about, Alec. He killed once and he'll kill again unless you remove him from society and give him the punishment he deserves."

"Great," Alec moaned. "My mother has turned into Dirty Harry."

"At least Dirty Harry had the balls to do what was right."

"Dirty Harry was a loose cannon, Ma. And he didn't exist," he added when Chase crooked an eyebrow at him.

"I liked his approach," Gran insisted. "Him and Charles Bronson. They knew what they were doing. Nowadays cops are too soft. Letting gangsters like this Drood fella walk."

"I'm not letting him walk!"

"You're gonna."

Odelia, who'd been following the conversation with half an ear, suddenly thought she was seeing things. On the windowsill an orange cat had just jumped up who looked a lot like Max. Then, as she watched, a second cat joined him, also orange and Max's spitting image. But it was only when a third cat joined the fray that she realized she wasn't dreaming, but that Max and Dooley were actually right there, and so was Max's twin.

Max was gesturing with his paw, opening his mouth and saying stuff she couldn't hear. It was obvious he wanted her to open the window and let them in. Problem was, Chase was sitting right next to the window, and he'd probably think it weird that she suddenly allowed three cats into Uncle Alec's office.

Alec had noticed the cats, too, for he frowned at them, then seemed to come to the same conclusion Odelia had reached. He had no qualms about Chase thinking whatever he was going to think, though, for he said, "Chase. Open that window, will ya?"

Only now did Chase notice the three cats. If he was surprised, he didn't show it. Being around Odelia he probably had gotten used to seeing cats wherever he went.

"Odelia," said Max the moment the window opened, "this guy here saw the killer!"

Odelia couldn't very well start talking feline in front of Chase, so she merely smiled when Max hopped down from the window and stalked over to her, rubbing himself against her leg. "His name is Big Mac. Don't ask. It's a long story. Literally. Anyway, I told him to come down here to look at some mugshots for you guys. And I promised he could get all the pizza he wanted if he did. That all right with you? He likes barbecue chicken pizza."

Odelia thought for a moment. How was she going to handle this?

Gran, who was sitting right next to her, suddenly piped up, "Alec. Could you be a doll and order me some barbecue chicken pizza? I'm having one of them midnight cravings."

Alec suppressed a smile. He knew the drill. "Chase, buddy? Do you mind?"

"On it," said Chase, being a real trooper. He took out his phone.

"Could you go and get it yourself, though?" said Alec, exchanging a quick glance with Odelia.

Chase laughed. "You're kidding, right? Domino's delivers, dude."

"I don't like Domino's," said Gran, and Chase's smile vanished.

"Yeah, she doesn't like Domino's," Uncle Alec echoed. "She likes…"

"Giovannini's," said Gran promptly. "And Giovannini's doesn't do home delivery."

Chase looked like he was going to say something, but one look at Gran's implacable face taught him otherwise. He got up. "Just the pizza, Mrs. Muffin?" he asked.

"And a Diet Coke," Gran nodded.

"If you're going all out I wouldn't mind some buffalo wings," said Big Mac.

"And buffalo wings," Gran added.

"And some creamy ranch chicken wings," said Big Mac.

"And some creamy ranch chicken wings," said Gran.

There was a momentary silence while Chase processed this. "That's it?" he asked.

Gran looked at Max.

Max looked at Big Mac.

Big Mac shook his head.

Max shook his head.

Gran said, "That's it, buckaroo. Off you go. Chop, chop."

CHAPTER 15

hen I was sure I had everyone's attention, I launched into my explanation on how we met Big Mac and what contribution this new best friend of ours could make to the investigation. Odelia listened with rapt attention and so did Gran. Even Uncle Alec seemed to hang on my every word—even though he probably didn't understand a thing I said.

When finally I was done, Odelia looked properly impressed.

"Great work, Max. So you really saw someone enter the library, Big Mac?"

Big Mac nodded. "Yes, I did, Miss Poole. In fact I saw several people enter that library."

Odelia relayed this information to her uncle, who was even more impressed than Odelia and her grandmother. Not for the first time the cats had saved the day. I hoped.

"So how are we going to do this?" the Chief asked, rubbing those sideburns again. "I mean, your cat buddy claims he saw several people enter the premises. Can he describe them?"

"I was hoping he could look at some mugshots," I said. "Isn't that how it's done?"

"Before we can have Big Mac look at mugshots we need to have some idea about who he saw," said Odelia. "Otherwise we'll be here all night."

"We'll be here all week," said Uncle Alec. "And if my officers discover I've been showing mugshots to a darn cat they'll call the loony bin and those jokers will have me in a straitjacket in no time."

"Oh, don't be such a pussy, Alec," said Gran. "Who cares what those losers think about you? If I paid attention to what people say behind my back I'd go nuts."

Uncle Alec's face, always on the ruddy side, had taken on a darker hue. He resembled one of those cartoon steam engines about to pop. "I'm the chief of police of this here town, Ma, so excuse me if I care about my reputation. It's my job that's on the line, not yours."

Since Grandma didn't really have a job, apart from helping out her son-in-law by playing receptionist at the doctor's office, I was curious to hear what she'd have to say about that. Dooley and Big Mac and I turned our heads back to Gran, almost like at a tennis match.

"Man up!" said Gran. "This cat risked life and limb to give you this most interesting witness testimony and all you can think about is your reputation? Give me a break."

Uncle Alec's face was now puce. It didn't become him.

"Let's all settle down," said Odelia, always the peace-keeper. "We're on the same page here. Now what we need to figure out is how to go about this thing."

"Preferably before Chase returns," the Chief muttered. "With a barbecue chicken pizza and side of straitjacket."

Odelia turned to Big Mac, who'd been following the altercation intently. "Tell us about these people you saw. Can you describe them?"

Big Mac scrunched up his face. It was obvious he was thinking hard. "Um, well, there was the pizza guy, like I told Max."

"Pizza guy," Odelia translated for Uncle Alec's sake.

"Which explains the pizza box we saw," Alec said, nodding.

"Only there was something weird about him," Big Mac said.

"In what way?" asked Odelia.

Big Mac shrugged. "He didn't smell like no pizza guy to me."

Cats have a very powerful sense of smell. In fact their sense of smell is about fourteen times stronger than a human's. Which means we can smell pizza a mile away.

Odelia decided to ignore the pizza comment. Big Mac obviously was very choosy when it came to his pizza. "So who else did you see?" she asked.

"Did you see this guy?" asked Uncle Alec, who seemed anxious to speed things up. He produced an actual mugshot and showed it to Big Mac, who eagerly nodded.

"Yup. I definitely saw him. He smelled like stale beer and dirty socks. Very icky."

"Sasha Drood," said Odelia, locking eyes with her uncle, who nodded.

"Oh, and then there was a guy who smelled like some type of expensive cologne," said Big Mac. "He was dressed in a fancy suit, too, and had a head like a potato."

"That sure narrows it down," said Gran.

I think she was being ironic, because Odelia didn't look pleased. But then Odelia got a great idea. She's like that. Always coming up with great ideas. "Why don't we get the sketch artist in here? She can work with Big Mac and whip us up some sketches?" When she saw the expression on her uncle's face she reconsidered. "Though that would probably buy you a one-way ticket to that loony bin, right?"

"At the very least," said Uncle Alec. "I'd probably be the laughingstock of the whole town, too, not to mention I'd lose my job and maybe even my pension."

"So… why don't *I* work with the sketch artist?" Odelia suggested next. "Big Mac could be sitting right next to me while I relay what he tells me to the artist. That way we'd skip any possible embarrassment or unwanted consequences."

Alec looked doubtful. "You'd have to come forward as a witness. Which you can't, as you were out on a date with Chase at the time this all went down."

"I could do it," said Gran. "I was there. And people think I'm nuts anyways."

This solution to the problem seemed to please Uncle Alec. Whether it was the part about his mother being nuts or the crime-solving possibilities the scheme offered wasn't entirely clear. "I like it," he said. "In fact I like it a lot." He turned to Big Mac. "Would you be willing to come in in the morning to work with our sketch artist, Big Mac?"

The big cat pondered this for a moment. "Do I get another pizza if I do?"

"Of course you do," said Gran. "You can have as much pizza as you want, little man."

I wondered how Uncle Alec was going to justify this sudden expenditure but I was pretty sure he'd find a way. Any police chief worth his salt is also a crafty bureaucrat.

The Chief scratched his scalp as he leaned back. "This is a first, people. Never in the history of law enforcement has a cat worked with the police to create a facial composite."

"There's got to be a first for everything," said Gran philosophically.

"Amen to that," said Odelia, who looked relieved that things were going to work out.

Just then, the door opened and Chase walked in, carrying a pizza box that simply smelled heavenly. I think we were all hungry, because the moment he set the box down on the desk, three pairs of human eyes and three pairs of cat's eyes all turned a little misty.

Big Mac must have sensed what we were all thinking, for he said loudly, "Hey! That pizza is mine! All mine!"

And then that wonderful boyfriend of Odelia's produced three more boxes of pizza from behind his back and said, "Ta-dah! I figured that after the night we've had we could all use a little pick-me-up, not just Mrs. Muffin."

I swear to God. Never had I loved a human being more than at that moment.

CHAPTER 16

hase let himself drop down on his recliner in Chief Alec's living room. Actually the room was living room, dining room and family room all in one. Being a widower, Alec didn't need a lot of space. It was surprisingly neat, though, given the fact that it now housed two dudes. And that was what Chase wanted to talk to his boss, mentor and housemate about.

"Want a beer?" asked Alec from the kitchen as he rooted around in the fridge.

"Nah, thanks," said Chase as he stared before him, going over the events of the evening. First his date with Odelia that had gotten off to such a good start, only to fizzle during dessert, just because some lowlife had decided taking Chris Ackerman's wallet, phone, watch and money wasn't enough —he had to take the poor sucker's life, too.

Chase didn't doubt for a second that they caught the right guy. So why the Chief would want Odelia's grandmother to come in tomorrow to sit with the sketch artist he did not know. Tying up loose ends, probably. Creating a solid case against Sasha Drood. Then again, if Grandma Muffin had indeed seen Drood enter the library around the time of the murder, why did she need to work with a sketch artist? There were obviously wheels within wheels at work here, and he thought he saw the hidden hand of Odelia in all of this.

Whenever cats were involved, and weird stuff he couldn't comprehend, usually Odelia was behind it. He didn't mind. This was a small town, and small towns worked in strange and wonderful ways. Like the fact that the chief of police would allow his niece to give him a hand investigating a crime. You didn't see that kind of thing back in New York.

Alec joined him and plunked his rotund frame into his own designated Barcalounger. The two recliners had been set up next to one another in front of the humongous flatscreen, like a matching pair. They practically looked like an old married couple, Chase thought.

"What a day," said the police chief, blowing out a sigh, then taking a sip of beer.

"At least we got our guy," said Chase, leaning his head back against the support.

"Let's not jump to conclusions, Detective Kingsley," grumbled the Chief. "I'm not convinced he's not what he says he is: a common robber."

"Pretty sure he's our guy," Chase insisted. He ticked off on his fingers. "We placed him at the scene. He's obviously a no-good thug who wouldn't mind adding murder to his rap sheet if it meant he could pocket a small fortune. Nah. He's our doer. No doubt about it."

The Chief studied Chase for a moment, then asked, "So how did your date go?"

Chase groaned. "I was just about to pop the question when you called."

"Sorry about that."

Chase waved a hand. "Not your fault. She got a call from

her mother at the same time I got a call from you. Besides, maybe it's too soon. Maybe she's just not ready yet."

"Or maybe she is, and all you have to do is ask her and she'll say yes."

"Your mother just moved out."

"So? Better strike the iron while it's hot. Knowing Vesta she and Tex will have another blowup and she'll move back in with Odelia before the end of the week." He stabbed a stubby finger in his direction. "You better move quick, son, before that happens."

Chase thought about this. "So… how should I go about it? Any advice for a desperate man?"

"The woman is crazy about you, son, that's pretty obvious. So from where I'm sitting you can't do no wrong."

Chase had a feeling he could go wrong in about a million different ways. He was fearless as a crime fighter but when it came to wooing Odelia Poole he was as nervous as a first-grader on his first day of school. "Do you think I should talk to Tex first? He is her dad, after all, and I want to do this right."

The Chief seemed to suppress a quick smile, but agreed this would be a great idea.

"I mean, things are done differently out here in Hampton Cove. Traditional, I mean."

"You got that right, son. We're big on tradition out here in the sticks."

He couldn't tell whether Alec was making fun of him or not but at least the other man hadn't shot down his idea about talking to Tex. He made up his mind to do just that the first chance he got. To his recollection he and the good doctor had never had a conversation about Odelia. Now was the time to correct that mistake. If he wanted to become a permanent part of Odelia's life he needed to create a strong bond with her family—starting with her dad.

"You know? While you're at it you might want to talk to Vesta, too," said the Chief.

"Now I know you're pulling my leg," he said, and when Alec's voluminous frame started shaking with rollicking laughter he knew he was right. Soon he was laughing right along with the big guy.

Next Alec would tell him to ask Odelia's cat for permission, too. Ha ha ha.

CHAPTER 17

*I*f you thought we were going beddy-bye after the long evening we'd had you're sorely mistaken. Cats don't go beddy-bye in the middle of the night. We go beddy-bye in the middle of the day. Nighttime is cattime so Dooley and I were still rearing to go-go-go!

Well, maybe not all that much. That hike to the Golden Arches and back had taken a toll on us. Still, there was still cat choir to attend, and no Hampton Cove feline wants to miss cat choir when they can help it. Not to sing, of course, but to socialize and sniff some butts. Not me, obviously. I'm not a butt-sniffer. But lots of my feline brethren and sistern are.

You can take a cat out of a butt but you can't take a butt out of a cat.

We'd said our goodbyes to Big Mac and headed off to Hampton Cove Park, where cat choir holds its nocturnal rehearsal sessions under the tutelage of Shanille, our conductor. When we arrived the place was already buzzing, and Dooley and I quickly joined Brutus and Harriet, who had secured themselves a spot near the benches. Cat choir rehearsals are held at the playground section of the park, us cats occupying the jungle gym and other multi-colored paraphernalia. My favorite spot is on top of the slide. I love sliding down the thing from time to time. It seems to help reaching both those low notes *and* the high ones.

Milo, our across-the-street neighbor's cat, who'd recently spent some time with us while his owner was vacationing in Florida, was also there. I was glad to see him. Before he met us his human never let him go outside. Odelia had had a little chat with Mrs. Lane and now Milo enjoyed that rare and wonderful privilege of the cat flap, without a doubt one of the greatest inventions made by man.

"Hey, buddy," I said when I spotted Milo.

"Max," he said with a nod.

Milo is a small, white cat with a very big imagination.

"Have you lost weight?" he asked now.

I was inordinately pleased. "You think so?" I asked, checking my girth.

"Your belly used to drag across the ground like a pot-bellied pig's and now it doesn't. That's how I can tell that you lost weight. Either that or your legs have gotten longer, which seems improbable."

My smile had vanished. I should have mentioned that Milo has a habit of insulting people—and cats. It stems from his days at the pound, when he had to fend for himself. You've got to be tough to survive life at the pound, and tough is Milo's middle name.

"I see you're still your usual, charming self," I grumbled.

"Hey, if it ain't broke, don't fix it." He directed a nod at Dooley, who was looking up at the heavens with a suspicious look on his face, as if expecting the sky to drop on his head.

"What's he looking at?" asked Milo curiously.

"Dooley has started watching the Discovery Channel—"

"Good for him."

"—and saw a documentary about the apocalypse. Climate change, Yellowstone, earth-destroying comets, the usual. And now he expects the world to end any moment."

"You're right, you know, Dooley," said Milo seriously.

Dooley looked over, surprised. "I'm right?"

Oh, God. *Here we go again*, I thought. Did I also mention Milo is a fantasist?

Milo placed a paw on Dooley's shoulder. "The world is ending tomorrow night at midnight on the dot. Which is why I'm feeling slightly maudlin." He transferred his paw to his heart. "And why I'm so glad I met you guys. True friendship is the only thing that makes this painful moment in our planet's existence worth living through."

"Oh, Milo," said Dooley, touched.

"Thanks for your friendship, Dooley," Milo said with a catch in his voice. "And you, Max. And Brutus and Harriet. I love you guys."

"How—how is the world ending, exactly?" asked Dooley. "Is it… Yellowstone? Is she finally going to blow? Or are the North Koreans launching those ICBMs of theirs? Or, or, or is it the three-hundred-foot tsunami that's going to wipe out the entire continent?"

"All of the above and more, Dooley," said Milo sadly.

"Wow."

"Yeah."

"That's…"

"I know."

Both cats were silent for a moment, taking a minute to process these truths, while Harriet rolled her eyes. Then again, if it wasn't on *The Bachelor*, Harriet didn't believe it.

"You can still save yourself, though, Dooley," said Milo now.

Hope surged in Dooley's eyes. "How?"

"Simple. Just kick a friend."

"Kick a friend?"

"Kick him hard. If everyone kicks a friend we can stop this apocalypse."

"Kick a friend," said Dooley thoughtfully.

"Here, let me show you," said Milo, and kicked Dooley.

"Hey!"

"Do you feel it?"

Dooley stared at the cat. "Feel what?"

"That surge of energy. If we all start kicking each other we elevate the planet's energy level. Once the planet's core energy signature changes, we collectively enter the sixth dimension and as everybody knows the apocalypse can't materialize in the sixth dimension."

"Huh," said Dooley, and eyed me curiously. I could see that his right leg was itching to give me a kick so I moved back a little.

A small smirk appeared on Milo's face so I gave him a warning glance.

'What?' his expression said.

'Cut it out,' my expression returned.

'I was just having a bit of fun.'

'You had your fun now cut it out.'

'Oh, all right. You're such a party pooper.'

Better be a party pooper than have cat choir turn into a kickfest. As we waited for Shanille to take up her position on top of the jungle gym and start rehearsals, I noticed how Brutus suddenly seemed to have disappeared.

"Where's Brutus?" I asked Harriet.

"Beats me," said Harriet. She didn't look happy. As if something was bugging her. "He's been acting weird all week," she added, then lowered her voice. "I think he's having an affair, Max."

"That's impossible. That cat is crazy about you."

"He was—now he's not."

"I think you're wrong. I happen to know Brutus very well and—"

"If you know him so well you'll know that he's been unusually quiet and maudlin."

I gave her a look of surprise. Not because of Brutus but because she knew the word maudlin.

"Maybe you should talk to him, Max. Man to man, I mean. He might tell you what's going on." Her expression hardened. "And if he's been having an affair I can tell you right now that I'll rip him to shreds and stomp on his remains then spit on his cheating carcass."

I gulped. Harriet can be fierce, and I didn't doubt for a moment she meant every word she said. "I'll talk to him," I promised. "In fact I'll do it right now." If I could find him, that was. "Can you keep an eye on Dooley? Milo's been filling his ears with nonsense again."

"I know. If he keeps it up I'll rip him to shreds, too, then stomp on—"

"His remains. I get it."

I was quick to put some distance between myself and Harriet. When she was in one of her moods there was no telling who'd be on the receiving end of those sharp claws.

To my surprise, I found Brutus hobnobbing with Shanille near a cluster of evergreens. The two of them were deep in conversation. So deep, in fact, that they didn't hear me sneak up on them until I was close enough to catch some snatches of what they were discussing.

"Come tonight and come alone," Shanille was saying.

"I will," Brutus responded, uncharacteristically solemn. "Are you sure about this, Shanille?"

"Of course I'm sure. But it's imperative that you tell no one, you hear?"

"Do you think I want anyone to know? I haven't even told Max, and he's my best bud."

I was so surprised to hear Brutus refer to me as his best bud that I accidentally stepped on a twig and it snapped. Both Shanille and Brutus looked up and spotted me.

"Hey, guys," I said with faux cheer. "Great weather we've been having, huh?"

Shanille shook her head disgustedly, then said, "You fix this, Brutus." She stalked off, leaving me and Brutus to stare at each other, an uncomfortable silence stretching out between us.

Finally, Brutus said, "There's something I need to tell you, Max."

I steeled myself for the big reveal. "I like Shanille."

He frowned. "What's that got to do with anything?"

"Nothing," I hastened to say. "Just a comment in the margin."

He took a deep breath, closed his eyes and said in a soft voice, "I'm dying, Max."

CHAPTER 18

"*W*ait, what?"

He nodded sadly. "Come here."

I came there—reluctantly.

He spread a few hairs on his chest. "See?"

Honestly I didn't see a thing. Mainly because it was pretty dark where we were standing, and also because Brutus is the color of the night: blacker than black.

"What am I looking at?" I asked finally.

"The spots. Can't you see them?"

"What spots?"

"The red spots!"

I squinted, straining my eyes and leaning in.

And this is how Dooley found us: me with my nose practically touching Brutus's chest.

"Guys?" he asked. "Am I interrupting something?"

"He's dying," I said without preamble.

In response, Dooley came over and gave Brutus a kick against the rear end.

"Hey!" Brutus cried, jerking up. "What was that for?"

"Do you feel it?" asked Dooley, wide-eyed.

"Of course I felt it. You kicked me!"

"Now you're in the sixth dimension and you won't die."

Brutus's jaw dropped. It wasn't a pretty sight. Finally, he reeled it back in and growled, "If you kick me one more time, I swear to God, I'll kick you so hard your backside will become your new face and you'll wear your tail as a nose."

Dooley gulped at this. Milo probably hadn't told him that even in the sixth dimension cats wouldn't enjoy being kicked up the backside.

"Have you told Marge or Odelia?" I asked.

"About the sixth dimension?" asked Dooley.

I ignored Dooley. "Someone should take a look at those spots."

"I've told Shanille and now I've told you and Justin Tucker over there."

"Who's Justin Tucker?" asked Dooley.

We both ignored him. Brutus was still sitting with his chest out and now I finally saw the spots. They were tiny and they were red. I didn't like the look of them, to be honest.

"I'm afraid that if I tell Odelia or Marge they'll take me to Vena and she'll say I've got cancer and will put me down on the spot. I don't want to be put down on the spot, Max."

"I understand." I did. No cat likes to be put down on the veterinarian's table. It's humiliating, not to mention unpleasant. We all want to die in our sleep after living a long and happy life. And be disease-free right up to the end. And stay far away from the vet.

Dooley, who'd been staring at Brutus's chest for the past five minutes, now said, "You have spots on your chest, Brutus."

Brutus muttered something I won't repeat here, seeing as children and senior citizens might be reading about my adventures, too. Suffice it to say it was the verbal equivalent of Dooley's sixth-dimension-inducing kick.

"So why Shanille?" I asked the sixty-four-thousand-dollar question.

"She's a religious cat," said Brutus. "I figured she would have some answers for me. And she did. She says I should invite Jesus into my life and he will heal me. She's scheduled for me to get baptized tomorrow night in the baptismal font over at St. John's Church. I'm going to do it, Max," he added when I gave him a slightly skeptical look.

"Maybe she can wash off those red spots while she's at it," said Dooley. He moved to touch Brutus's chest. "Is that paint or tomato sauce?"

"Don't touch my spots," said Brutus, deftly evading Dooley's grabbing paw.

"Don't touch his spots, Dooley," I said. "They could be contagious."

This was the right approach. Dooley's paw froze mid-air. "Contagious?" he asked in a strangled, squeaky voice. "You mean… you're really dying? Like, dying-from-a-contagious-disease dying?"

"You don't have to rub it in," Brutus growled.

Dooley immediately retracted his paw and took a few steps back. Dooley has a thing about dying and diseases. He doesn't like them. He opened and closed his mouth a few times, a look of panic in his eyes. "I want to get baptized, too —but I get to go first!" he now exclaimed.

"Don't tell me. You're afraid Brutus will contaminate the baptismal font," I said wearily.

Dooley nodded fifteen times in quick succession. "I'm going first!"

Looked like Dooley had found Jesus, too. Well, it was only a matter of time.

"Will you come with me, Max?" asked Brutus, giving me a pleading look.

"Of course I will," I told the other cat. "I draw the line at holding your paw, though."

Brutus laughed, though I could tell he'd been hoping I would hold his paw.

"So I go first, then Max, then Brutus," said Dooley, who had it all figured out.

"Wait, what?" I said. "I'm not getting baptized, you guys."

"Why not? The world is ending tomorrow night, Brutus is dying. What do you have to lose?"

"I'm sorry, but I'm not into religion." In fact the only church I prayed at was the church of Cat Snax. Now there was something I believed in.

"These are desperate times, Max," said Dooley, switching to seasoned preacher mode. "And desperate times call for desperate measures. Do you really want to risk your soul burning in hell for all of eternity? Or do you want to join me and Brutus in cat heaven?"

"What does cat heaven look like, exactly?" asked Brutus, interested.

"No idea," said Dooley. "You have to ask Shanille. She's the expert."

And so she was. "What about Harriet?" I asked. "Shouldn't we tell her?"

"No, don't tell her, Max," Brutus urged me. "She'll be devastated."

"She'll be more devastated when you die without telling her."

"That's the whole point, isn't it?" asked Brutus with more than a little heat. "I hope I won't die. I hope Shanille will heal me."

"I thought you said Jesus would heal you," said Dooley, puzzled.

"I don't care who heals me!" Brutus cried. "As long as someone does!"

"Keep your shirt on, Brutus," I said, which probably didn't make sense. Cats don't wear shirts. Dogs do, but then we all know dogs are idiots.

"I'm desperate here, Max, can't you see?" said Brutus, and I had to admit I'd never seen him quite as unraveled as this.

I could tell I was going to have to hold his paw. And Dooley's. I was going to be the official pawholder of our little band of three. I didn't mind. I liked Brutus. He'd grown on me ever since he'd come to live with us. If holding his paw got rid of his red spots I was all for it.

Brutus looked down. Dooley's paw had surreptitiously slipped against his own. Brutus looked up, giving Dooley a look that could kill. Dooley produced a sheepish smile.

"I figured since we're going to be Jesus buddies, we might hold paws," he said.

Brutus lifted his upper lip in a snarl, and Dooley quickly removed his paw.

Brutus might be covered in red spots, but he'd lost none of his bite.

CHAPTER 19

$\mathcal{N}$ine o'clock on the dot the next morning Odelia and Gran strode into Uncle Alec's office. Chase and the Chief were already present, and they were accompanied by a young woman with long bright pink hair and denim overalls over a Calvin & Hobbes T-shirt.

"Odelia—Ma—this is Lara Dun. She works for the Suffolk County Police Department. We have her on loan for the day so make sure you don't waste her time."

With these words, he directed a pointed look at Big Mac, who was safely ensconced in Odelia's arms, and Max, who was being carried by Gran.

Chase, when he noticed that both Gran and Odelia had come bearing cats, gave them a look of surprise.

"Oh, you brought your cats," said Lara, and got up to give Max a cuddle. He had the good decency to purr in response.

"So where's the pizza?" asked Big Mac, as he wriggled in Odelia's arms.

"Work first, food later," said Max, and Odelia couldn't have expressed it better.

"Why don't you use my office?" said Uncle Alec. "No one

will disturb you here," he added with a knowing look at his niece.

Chase got the hint, for he filed out of the room, followed by the Chief, who closed the door behind him.

"So how do you want to do this?" asked Odelia.

"Just take a seat and I'll be over here doing my thing," said Lara with a bright smile. She seemed like a sweet young woman. She took a seat, one leg tucked underneath her bum, and positioned a large sketch pad on her knee, a pencil in her hand, and sat poised.

Odelia and Gran sat across from the sketch artist while Big Mac and Max sat at their feet.

"So you saw several people enter the library last night, right?" said Odelia.

"That's right," said Big Mac.

"Uh-huh," said Gran.

"How many people would you say you saw?"

Big Mac thought hard. "Um, seven. Eight if you count the pizza guy."

"Eight," Gran announced.

"Let's go through the list," said Odelia.

And so they did. Big Mac shared his recollections with them, Gran passed them on as her own, and Lara quietly worked away. It took quite a while to produce composites of all the people who'd visited the library that night. The morning passed quickly, and by the time Uncle Alec waltzed in, carrying three pizza boxes and placing them on the desk, seven sketches were the end result of the long session. The pizza guy was the only one Big Mac hadn't been able to describe, as he'd been wearing a ball cap and the cat had been watching the pizza more than the deliverer. They would check all the pizza parlors and get the name of the delivery guy. Or, better yet, check Ackerman's phone to see what parlor he'd called.

"So?" asked Uncle Alec, planting his hands on the desk. "How did it go?"

Lara handed him the sketches and he frowned as he went through them. "Huh. Now all we gotta do is figure out who these people are."

"Can I take a look?" asked Odelia.

Alec handed her the pictures while he placed one of the pizza boxes on the floor and watched as Big Mac dug in with relish and a fervor that elicited chuckles from everyone present. He was a great little eater. Well, maybe little wasn't the right word to describe him.

Odelia flipped through the sketches. "Nice work," she said. "These are amazing."

"Thanks," said Lara with a smile. "You gave me so much detail to work with it wasn't hard. You're very perceptive, Mrs. Muffin. I don't think I've ever met someone with as good an eye for detail as you."

"Yeah, well," said Gran. "It's a gift."

"Under the circumstances your eyesight is simply amazing. Your son told me that there's only one lamp at the back of the library, and it doesn't even give a lot of light."

Gran adjusted her glasses. "I've always had great eyesight. Some people say I have the eyes of a cat."

Lara laughed at this. "If you had cat's eyes that would explain how you pulled this off." She rose to her feet and held out her hand. "It's been a pleasure working with you. And you, Miss Poole. Usually people don't remember half of what you remembered. I had fun."

"It was so nice meeting you," Odelia said gratefully.

Lara walked out and Gran puffed out her chest. "I like that girl. She knows her stuff. The things she said about my eyesight and my powers of observation confirmed I've got what it takes to be an ace detective."

"You do realize she was unknowingly complimenting Big Mac, don't you?" said Odelia.

"Let's not split hairs," said Gran.

Odelia, who'd picked up the sketches again, tapped one depicting a man with sunken eyes and a square chin. "Isn't this Rockwell Burke? The horror writer?"

Gran squinted at the sketch. "Dang it. I forgot my reading glasses."

So much for her amazing cat-like eyesight.

"We better show these to Mom," said Odelia. "She's always been Chris Ackerman's biggest fan. If these people are associated with Ackerman, she might recognize them."

And so she did. Fifteen minutes later Marge Poole joined them, and another ten minutes later she'd identified four out of seven.

"That's Ackerman's wife. I think her name is Angelique. That's Ackerman's son Trey. That's Rockwell Burke—weird. I thought he hadn't shown up. Um, and that's Malcolm Buckerfield. Like I told you before, he is—or was—Ackerman's publisher." She stared at the final three sketches but shook her head. "I've never seen these. Maybe they're more of Ackerman's relatives?"

"That's Sasha Drood," said Uncle Alec. "He's the one who stole Ackerman's valuables. He might be the one who killed him."

Mom pressed her lips together in disapproval. "What a nasty, nasty man. Even if he didn't actually kill Chris Ackerman he did something that's almost just as bad. You don't steal from a dead man."

"Or a dying man," said Odelia softly. The thought hadn't occurred to her before, but if what Drood said was true, and he hadn't actually killed Ackerman, he might have watched him die, and hadn't lifted a finger to help him. She frowned and turned to her uncle. "If Drood is telling the truth, then he must have arrived just after Ackerman was killed. In which case he might have seen the killer."

"I asked him that same question. He says he didn't see anyone."

"He could be lying to protect the killer."

Uncle Alec agreed that that was a distinct possibility.

"Hey, this pizza is amazing!" Big Mac cried from his position on the floor. When Odelia looked, she saw that the pizza was gone.

"Max? Did you get to eat something?" she asked.

Max shook his head. "I figured Big Mac deserved the whole thing."

And so he did. Two more pizzas were sitting on the desk. She picked up a slice and placed it down in front of Max. "This is for you," she said warmly. "You brought us Big Mac. You deserve a treat just as much as he does."

"Yes, you did great, Max," said Marge, and Gran confirmed that Max was a real trooper. Uncle Alec merely grinned. Even though he'd heard his mother, his sister and his niece talk feline all his life, it never failed to elicit a smile from the big guy.

CHAPTER 20

*O*nce Odelia had dropped Big Mac off at Mickey D's and picked up Dooley from the house, it was time for us to conduct our first interview on the Baffling Case of the Murdered Best-Selling Author of the World. As all self-respecting sleuths know, interviews are a detective's bread and butter. It's what we live for. Read any Hercule Poirot or Miss Marple novel and it's wall-to-wall interviews. Some people think it gets a little boring after a while, but not me. Oh, no. I love chatting with suspects. Getting under their skin. Making them talk!

Only problem is, most suspects don't speak cat. But I don't mind. I talk to their pets instead, and boy, oh, boy do pets have the most fascinating stories to share. Often they know more about humans and their weird and quirky ways than the humans themselves!

And so it was that Odelia steered her decrepit old Ford in the direction of downtown Hampton Cove, me and Dooley in the back and Grandma Muffin riding shotgun. Usually it's Chase who's Odelia's preferential sleuthpartner, but I guess family comes first. And since Chase wasn't family yet, Gran had effectively managed to usurp the cop's position.

"So before we go in there we need to establish a few ground rules," said Odelia as the car hurtled through town, belching out fumes and rattling as if something was going to bust loose any minute now. A hubcap, maybe, or a vital piece of engine. "One. We behave professionally, which means we don't pretend to be cops, and we always stay polite."

"Too bad. I figured we'd do good cop, bad cop and I'd get to be the bad cop," said Gran.

"Second, better let me ask the questions. I've done this before and I know how to handle myself."

"Honey, I've done this a thousand times before. I'm old!" she added when Odelia gave her a skeptical look. "I've talked people into saying stuff they didn't want to say from way before you were even born. Men, mostly, but women, too." She looked grim. "You wouldn't believe the things I got your grandfather to confess when I used my thumbscrews on him."

Odelia laughed, but then seemed to realize Gran wasn't kidding. She cleared her throat. "Three. We find a way to insert Max and Dooley into the room so they can talk to the suspects' pets. And we never, ever, leave them behind."

Never leave a fallen pet behind. I liked it. One of those rules to live by, huh?

"You don't have to tell me how to do my job," said Gran, holding up a hand. "I'm a born detective, sweetie. Put me in a room with a suspect and I can tell at a glance whether they did it or not." She tapped her nose. "It's called intuition and I've got it up the wazoo."

"Just… let me do the talking," said Odelia, who didn't seem comfortable with the idea of bringing her grandmother along for these interviews.

"So how did it go with Big Mac?" asked Dooley.

"It went great," I said. "He identified seven people who snuck into the library last night, and then Marge recognized four of them. Number five was the guy they picked up last night—the one who stole Mr. Ackerman's valuables and probably killed him, too. Number eight was a pizza guy, so that only leaves two more Uncle Alec needs to trace."

"If the thief is the killer, why are we even doing these interviews?" asked Dooley, and very correctly so, I should add.

"Because the thief says he didn't do it, and there's some debate about whether to believe him or not. Chief Alec thinks he didn't do it, and neither does Gran. Chase thinks he did it, and Odelia is on the fence."

"What do you think, Max?"

"I don't think anything. I'm a professional detective and professional detectives merely collect evidence then use deductive reasoning to come to a definite conclusion."

Dooley looked appropriately impressed. "Did you learn all that from the Hallmark Channel?"

"Amongst other things," I said smugly. I didn't tell him I'd recently rewatched *Sherlock Holmes 1* and *2* with Odelia and that had taught me a thing or two, too. Mainly that Jude Law is probably the most handsome man alive, and that Robert Downey Jr. does a very wonky British accent.

We'd arrived at the Hampton Cove Star hotel, across the street from Vickery General Store, where one of my main informants Kingman holds court. Which reminded me I should have a chat with Kingman. This thing with Brutus's spots had been worrying me and maybe Kingman had some old remedy to cure our friend. Some root or herb or whatever.

Odelia parked her car in a no-parking zone, then got out and Dooley and I followed suit. We trotted up to the hotel's entrance and Odelia picked us both up and carried us inside.

At least the Hampton Cove Star isn't one of those No Pets Allowed places. I hate it when hotels do that. There should probably be a law against that. The no No Pets law.

Gran had taken out her smartphone and was aiming it at Odelia.

"What are you doing?" asked Odelia.

"Filming you. What do you think I'm doing?"

"And why are you filming me?"

"For my vlog. Didn't I tell you? I have a vlog. It's like a blog, but less boring because it's got video. I've been filming lots of things. I filmed Tex while he was sleeping, and Marge while she was in the bathroom. I'm trying to paint a portrait of life as a middle-aged woman in the suburbs. I'm calling it *Desperate Housewives*."

"You can't use that title."

"Too bad. I already did."

"*Desperate Housewives* is a famous TV show, Gran."

"I'm sure it's not."

"Besides, you're not a middle-aged woman and Hampton Cove isn't the suburbs."

"You're just jealous because I thought of it first." She pointed her phone at us and Dooley and I stared up at her.

"Are we going to be in this movie, too, Gran?" asked Dooley.

"Of course you are. What would life for a desperate housewife be without her trusty pets? Now smile for the camera, you guys. Big smiles."

I could have told her that cats don't smile. Instead, we meowed. That seemed to satisfy her inner desperate housewife for she said, "Excellent," and tucked her phone away.

"You're not filming the suspects," said Odelia.

"Of course I'm filming the suspects. I filmed Drood, didn't I? And I filmed Ackerman—before *and* after he tumbled off his perch."

Odelia turned to her grandmother, looking absolutely horrified. "You didn't!"

Gran patted her phone. "This is going to be a very special episode of *Desperate Housewives*. The one where Vesta and Odelia solve the murder of a famous writer."

"You can't film our murder investigation! That's…" She flapped her arms like a desperate chicken. "Unethical not to mention people could sue for breach of privacy!"

"Poppycock. *Cops* does it all the time."

"They have people sign release forms!"

"I don't think so. People love to be on TV."

The elevator had arrived on the second floor and jerked to a stop. The doors slid open and we all walked out. My paws sunk into the plush carpet and I couldn't resist the urge to dig my claws in and do a little stropping. What? It was a very nice carpet!

Meanwhile, the *Desperate Housewives* feud was still ongoing.

"Gran," said Odelia warningly, "put away that phone. Now!"

"I'm a vlogging detective! I can't vlog without my phone!"

Odelia made a grab for Gran's phone, but the old lady deftly held it out of reach.

"Gimme that," Odelia grunted.

"Over my dead body," Gran returned.

"That can be arranged."

"You would strike your poor old grandmother?"

"I thought you were a desperate housewife?"

"You are being very rude, young lady," said Gran, trying a different tack.

Just then, the door Odelia had knocked on swung open, and a heavyset woman with curly gray hair and horse-faced features appeared. She didn't look happy to see us.

Immediately Odelia plastered a pleasant smile on her

face. "Mrs. Ackerman? My name is Odelia Poole and this is Vesta Muffin. We're civilian consultants working with the Hampton Cove Police Department and we would like to ask you a few questions about the death of your husband Chris Ackerman. May we come in?"

The woman's eyes shifted between Odelia and Gran. Finally, she asked gruffly, "Why are you filming me?"

"Police procedure, Mrs. Ackerman," said Gran swiftly. "To protect ourselves from potential lawsuits we've been legally advised to film any contact with the general public."

"Huh," said Mrs. Ackerman.

"Yup. Cops have body cameras. Civilian consultants have to make do with these."

"Weird," the woman commented, but then shrugged it off and bade us all entry.

CHAPTER 21

*O*delia didn't like Gran's latest obsession. This *Desperate Housewives* thing could jeopardize their entire investigation. Then again, Gran was a smooth talker. She could probably talk her way out of any jam. Years of diligently watching every single soap opera out there had equipped her with a battery of ready-made quips or strategems to get her out of trouble. At least Mrs. Ackerman had been so distracted by Gran's filming that she probably hadn't even noticed that Max and Dooley had inserted themselves into the room.

"Take a seat," Mrs. Ackerman said, gesturing at two chairs placed near the window. "This won't take long, I hope? I just lost my husband and I've got a funeral to plan."

She didn't exactly seem overwrought with grief. Then again, we all have different ways of dealing with loss, so maybe being businesslike about it was Mrs. Ackerman's way.

"This definitely won't take long," Odelia assured the other woman as she took a seat. "So where is your son? I thought you said over the phone he'd join us?"

"Trey!" Mrs. Ackerman bellowed. "Get in here!"

A connecting door opened and a lanky young man strode in. He had a pale, thin face and a buzzcut and looked more like a drug addict than any drug addict Odelia had ever met.

"This is Trey," said Mrs. Ackerman, indicating the young man. "Trey, these two are from the police, apparently."

"Thank you so much for your time, Mr. Ackerman," said Odelia.

"Have you found my father's murderer yet?" asked Trey, giving them a glum look.

"My uncle does have someone in custody," said Odelia. "My uncle is the chief of police."

"You made an arrest?" asked Mrs. Ackerman. "Why weren't we informed?"

"The guy didn't do it," said Gran, who'd placed her phone on the table, propped up against a potted mini-cactus, where it continued filming the scene.

Odelia gritted her teeth. "What Vesta means to say is that the person who was arrested denies all involvement. He does, however, admit that he stole certain valuables from Mr. Ackerman's person."

"Valuables? Like what?"

"Diamond watch, money, iPhone," said Gran. "That kind of stuff."

"The bastard," muttered Trey.

"Yeah, he's a piece of bad news, all right," Gran admitted. "But as far as I can tell he's not the killer."

"That's up to the prosecutor to decide," said Odelia pointedly. "What we're here to determine is if perhaps you noticed something last night when you went to visit your husband at the library?"

Mrs. Ackerman exchanged a quick glance with her son, who turned to look out the window, arms folded across his chest. His mother, meanwhile, plunked her heavy frame down on a settee and cast down her eyes. "You'll probably know this already, but my husband and I... we were in the process of getting a divorce."

Gran's eyes went wide, and she quickly cast a look at her phone. This was the stuff she wanted featured on *Desperate Housewives*. "A divorce?" she asked. "You mean he was involved with another woman?"

Mrs. Ackerman frowned, and so did Odelia. "As a matter of fact he was," said Mrs. Ackerman. "He was having an affair with his editor. She'd recently gotten a job at a different publisher and had enticed Chris to change publishers as well." She heaved a deep sigh. "My husband was about to embark on an entirely new life, Miss Poole. Without his wife of thirty years, and without the publisher responsible for his success. And all over a woman."

"Who's this editor?" asked Gran.

"Her name is Stacey Kulcheski."

"Is she staying in town?" asked Odelia.

"I don't think so. At least I haven't seen her."

"So why did you join your husband at the library last night?"

Mrs. Ackerman briefly wrung her hands. "I—I decided— we decided to try and talk to him one more time. He didn't even know we'd flown in. He was quite surprised when we suddenly turned up out of the blue. You see, my husband had stopped taking my calls."

"Our calls," her son corrected her.

"Our calls," said Mrs. Ackerman with a vague smile. "Ever since he packed up his things and walked out on us we'd had no way of getting in touch with him. So when Trey saw he was scheduled to speak at your local library, we decided to confront him."

"Talk some sense into him," Trey clarified. He turned to face them. "My father was under a spell. He didn't know what he was doing. This Kulcheski woman had hypnotized him."

"She had?" asked Gran.

"Not literally, Gran," Odelia murmured.

"Oh."

"She had him eating out of her hand—doing her bidding at every turn. We knew that the only way to break the spell was to lay it all out for him. Expose the woman as the wily little gold digger she was."

"And? How did he respond?" asked Odelia.

"Not well. He kicked us out. Said he never wanted to see us again."

"After all I'd done for him," said Mrs. Ackerman bitterly. "I stood by his side when he was a struggling author. I worked my butt off to keep our family afloat in the early years, when every submission ended in a flutter of rejection letters. If not for me he'd never have become a success. He'd have given up long ago. But I believed in him. I believed in his talent as a storyteller. It took him ten years to sell his first novel. And another ten to become a household name. And this is how he repaid me. By chasing the first skirt that came along."

"She wasn't the first skirt, Mom," said her son. "There were others."

"I could deal with that. We had an understanding. They were butterflies. I was his wife. The woman he came home to. Until he decided he no longer needed me."

Gran cleared her throat. "Do you have any idea who might have killed your husband, Mrs. Ackerman?"

Mrs. Ackerman raised her eyes to Gran. "You think I did it, don't you? And you're right."

Both Odelia and Gran held their breath. Was a confession coming?

Instead, Mrs. Ackerman said, "I *could* have killed him. I

know I was hopping mad when I left that library. But I'm not a killer. Instead I was going to take my husband to court and clean him out. I was prepared to make sure that he was left with nothing. That would have been my revenge."

"Very iffy proposition," said Gran. "Better to kill him and collect the inheritance."

Trey Ackerman's eyes flashed dangerously. "Are you accusing my mother of murder?"

"Just throwing it out there," said Gran. "If long experience as a homicide detective has taught me one thing it's that it's almost always the spouse that did it. So convince me otherwise. Prove your innocence, Mrs. Ackerman."

A quick smile flitted across the woman's face. "I don't have to prove my innocence. There's a man who can prove it for me. When Trey and I left Chris was still alive. Just ask Malcolm Buckerfield. He walked in as we walked out. And he had every reason to murder Chris. Without Chris, Buckerfield had nothing. Chris Ackerman *was* Buckerfield Publishing."

CHAPTER 22

*O*delia had signed us up to interrogate the suspects' and witnesses' pets and so that's what Dooley and I set out to do. Only as far as we could ascertain there were no pets in evidence. I did pick up a strange odor, though. It didn't belong to a cat or dog or any other animal I'd ever encountered. In fact it smelled oddly... floral.

We stealthily moved from the living room into the bedroom in search of our prey, but it was Dooley who finally discovered the anomaly. I call it an anomaly because it was the one animal I would never have advised any human to keep as a pet.

"Oink oink," said the anomaly.

We both stared at it. It was small, it was pink, it was cuddly, and it was looking at us through beady little eyes. Perched on the foot of the bed, it even had its own little basket.

"Oink oink," it repeated.

"What is it, Max?" asked Dooley.

"I think it's a... pig," I said.

"Oink oink."

"A pig? Are you sure?"

I wasn't. For that I needed to take a closer look. So I jumped on the bed and stared at the thing. It was a pig, all right. Round and pink and small. Not a pig. A piglet.

The piglet snuffled for a moment, seemingly interested in our sudden appearance.

"Hey, there," I said finally, when I'd gotten over my initial surprise.

"Hullo," said the pig, in a surprisingly deep voice for such a tiny creature.

"My name is Max," I said, "and this is Dooley."

"Is it safe to come up, Max?" asked Dooley from the floor.

I'd heard stories about pigs biting people, but this little dude didn't look like a biter. "Sure," I said therefore. "He looks like a nice piglet—are you a nice piglet, piglet?"

"Of course I'm a nice piglet, cat," growled the piglet. "We're all civilized here."

"You look awfully young," I said. "How old are you?"

"Three."

"Years?"

"Months."

"Huh."

"Yeah. I still have to get my growth spurt. Which I trust will kick in any day now."

"So are you—"

"A potbellied pig, yeah," he nodded. "Humans love us for our lovable yet surprisingly mature personalities and our positive outlook on life. How about you guys?"

"I'm four," said Dooley. "Years, not months."

"Me, too," I said.

"Humans love us for the cuddles," said Dooley. "Though they come back for the conversation."

The pig gave Dooley a dubious look, then said, "I'm Kevin Bacon, by the way, and this is Miss Piggy."

We looked up to see a second piglet, even pinker than the first one, waddle across the bed in our direction.

"Hey, you guys," said Miss Piggy. "Great to see you. I've never actually seen a cat up close before. Heard a lot about you, of course, but this is definitely a first for me. You don't bite, do you? Ha ha. Just kidding. I know you don't. Make yourselves comfortable and welcome to our humble abode."

Dooley and I stared at the newcomer. I'd never met a motormouth pig before, and it was fascinating to see how long she could continue talking without coming up for oxygen.

"So… we're actually here to talk about Chris Ackerman," I said, deciding to get down to business before Miss Piggy burst into speech again. Odelia and Gran were only going to be in here for so long, so we had a pretty strict deadline to adhere to.

"Who?" asked Kevin Bacon.

"Oh, you know, Kevin Bacon," said Miss Piggy. "He-Who-Must-Not-Be-Named."

"Oh, him," said Kevin Bacon, then shook his head. "We're not supposed to mention him. Or discuss him. Angelique gave us strict instructions, remember?"

"Angelique?" I said.

"Our human," Miss Piggy explained. "He-Who-Must-Not-Be-Named was her husband. Until he ran off with another woman. Now he's dead to us."

"He's actually really dead," said Kevin Bacon.

"He is," Miss Piggy confirmed. "Angelique told us this morning."

"Did Angelique also mention to you who killed Mr. Ackerman?" I asked.

"Karma," said Kevin Bacon.

"Who's Karma?" asked Dooley.

"Not who, what," I said. "Did she really say that?"

"Karma in action," Miss Piggy confirmed. "Said he got what he deserved. Well, she used slightly stronger language than that, but that's the gist of it. Angelique wasn't very fond of her husband. She used to be, but since he started boning a skirt half his age she wasn't. At least that's what she told us." She laughed. "I honestly have no idea what half the stuff she tells us means but there you have it in a nutshell. So why do you want to know about He-Who-Must-Not-Be-Named? Are you police cats or something? I've heard of police dogs but I've never heard of police cats. Though it stands to reason they would exist. Cats are pretty savvy, after all. Not that I would know. Like I said I've never met a cat before. Not in the flesh, I mean. But you look pretty savvy to me. At least one of you does."

She gave Dooley a hesitant look, as if fully expecting him to be upset, but Dooley was merely looking slightly dazed. Like me, he'd never met a talkative pig before either.

"We, um, we're actually working with our human," I said, after I'd remembered there was a question hidden amid the word diarrhea. "She's a police consultant and a reporter and she's trying to figure out who killed Chris Ack—He-Who-Must-Not-Be-Named."

Kevin Bacon and Miss Piggy shared a quick look of concern. "Oh, dear. This is going to bring Angelique to tears," said Miss Piggy. "She still has feelings for her ex-husband."

"I'm sure she doesn't," grunted Kevin Bacon.

"And I'm sure she does. She's been crying herself to sleep for weeks, Kevin Bacon, or haven't you heard?"

Her porcine helpmeet muttered something incomprehensible, then waddled off to the edge of the bed and jumped off onto the fluffy carpet below.

"He's very sensitive about our human's predicament," Miss Piggy whispered. "Ever since He-Who-Must-Not-Be-Named walked out on Angelique, Kevin Bacon has been suffering from heart palpitations. Sympathy symptoms, the vet says." She shook her head. "It's been a terrible, trying time. Hopefully the man's death will bring a measure of closure." She then plastered a cheerful expression onto her face. "So. Cats, huh? Tell me about those nine lives. What's your secret? Can you teach me? I mean, who doesn't want nine lives, right? Seriously, though. Tell me. I need to know."

"Um…" I said.

"Max, Dooley!" Odelia yelled from the other room.

"Sorry, Miss Piggy," I said, hopping down from the bed. "Time to go!"

"Hey!" she said. "You haven't told me your secret!"

"It's very simple," said Dooley. "A balanced diet, plenty of sleep, and try to stay out of trouble."

"That's your big secret? There's something you're not telling me, cat! Come back here!"

But we were already on our way out. We hadn't learned a thing in there, apart from the fact that pigs could be real chatty and that Angelique Ackerman had loved her husband.

I sure hoped that the next interview would land us a few more revelations. Then again, the true detective takes the bad with the good and knows that not every clue will lead to the killer. There will always be a few red herrings buried in there. Or pink piglets.

CHAPTER 23

*J*t was a nice concatenation of circumstances that Rockwell Burke was staying at the same hotel as Chris Ackerman's widow. It meant that Odelia and her entourage—consisting of her aged grandmother and two cats —didn't have to travel all the way out to Hampton Cove's billionaire lane, where all the rich people lived. Instead, they went one floor up to arrive at the boutique hotel's penthouse suite and knocked on the door.

Rockwell Burke himself opened the door, barefoot and dressed in tattered jeans and an equally tattered T-shirt that proclaimed he loved *The Walking Dead*. Not surprising as he was, after all, a famed horror novelist.

For a moment, Odelia was speechless. She was in the presence of greatness, not to mention one of her childhood heroes, as she'd practically grown up with the man's books. Lucky for her Gran had never suffered from being tongue-tied or diffident.

"Rockwell Burke?" she announced. "We're here to interrogate you about the murder of Chris Ackerman, the man you once called a hack writer and a fraud and who was found dead with a fountain pen up his jugular at a reading you were scheduled to officiate."

Rockwell rocked back on his heels, visibly shaken. "Who are you people? The cops?"

"Close enough," said Gran, and pushed her way into the room, past the horrormeister. Odelia, mortified, stood grinning up at the famous author, still speechless.

ф

"So who are these *Walking Dead*, Max?" asked Dooley when Odelia and Rockwell had finally moved inside and the writer had closed the hotel door, after watching me and Dooley stalk past him. The writer had the stunned look on his face of one who's come into contact with Gran. She would definitely make a great 'bad cop' if she ever chose to sign up.

"They're zombies," I said, checking around and observing that this room, even though it was called a penthouse suite, wasn't all that different from Angelique Ackerman's. The only difference was that it was bigger, and had a wraparound balcony that offered a nice view of Hampton Cove's main street down below.

"Zombies? You mean dead people who aren't really dead and like to snack on human brains?"

"Yup."

"But why would any human love zombies? Aren't they extremely dangerous?"

"I guess horror writers prefer undead humans over live ones. Undead humans don't leave bad reviews, after all."

"But they kill live humans!"

"Creating more undead humans, which is just a win-win for all. Do you see any pets in here?"

"I hope not," said Dooley with a shiver. "If they're all like that Miss Piggy I hope we don't run into any more pets on this particular tour of duty."

"Pity." Miss Piggy and Kevin Bacon were a washout, as far as sleuthing went. I was hoping to score some points with the next batch but it looked like Burke was not a pet lover.

So instead of wandering around in search of our next target, we settled down near the window, where the rays of the sun played on our fur and where it was nice and warm, and listened to Odelia and Gran conduct their second interview of the day.

"Isn't it true, Mr. Burke," said Gran in sharp tones, directing her phone at the horror writer, "that you hated Mr. Ackerman? And isn't it also true that you resented the fact that he made a lot more money at this writing thing than you did? And isn't it also true that—"

"Wait a minute," said Rockwell, holding up his hands in a gesture of defense. "I mean, it's true that I once said Ackerman wasn't much of a writer."

"You called him a hack."

"I meant it as a compliment! Ackerman was a writer in the pulp fiction tradition. He could produce a clean draft in next to no time, and his readers loved it. Where it took me a year to write a halfway decent book he wrote a dozen, and they sold like hot cakes."

"So you hated his guts," said Gran, narrowing her eyes.

"I admired him!"

"You were jealous!"

"No! Well, yeah, maybe a little. I mean, who wouldn't be? He sold more books than the next ten writers on the bestseller list. He raised the bar for all of us. Did I envy him? Sure! Did I want to kill him over his killer output? Of course not! I wanted to *be* him, not kill him."

"Hmph," Gran said, indicating she didn't believe a word the novelist said.

"Look, I went in there last night fully intending to set the record straight. I know I've said some things about Chris in the past that he was sore about, even though at the time I meant it in jest—like I said, more in tribute than criticism. My words got twisted and we ended up with this feud or whatever. So when my publisher suggested I moderate the reading I jumped at the chance. But when I got there I suddenly had a change of heart." He shook his head. "I—I worried that people would see this as a publicity stunt. My last couple of novels weren't well received, and my sales have been down. The only thing I've got going for me is that I've never sold out. My fans know I don't compromise. That I'll never go on TV to hawk a product or a book I don't believe in. And going into that reading suddenly felt like a bad idea. This business is about perception and I don't want to be accused of selling out."

"I'm sure your readers wouldn't have seen it that way," said Odelia gently. "They would have seen it for what it was: a writer not afraid to confess he made a mistake."

Rockwell smiled. "You're too kind, Miss Poole. But I doubt that in this social media age people would have taken my side. Pretty sure the pitchforks would have been out and a very public tarring and feathering would have ensued. My fans can be pretty darn vocal."

"So let me get this straight," said Gran. "You never went inside the library?"

"Oh, I went inside, all right. But the moment I did my gut told me it was all wrong. So I turned around and walked right out again."

"Without talking to Ackerman?"

"Without talking to Ackerman."

"He wasn't going to be happy about that."

"No, I'm sure he wasn't. But that couldn't be helped. My integrity means more to me than selling a few more books.

And as it happens it was probably a good thing that I walked. I would have gotten embroiled in this whole murder business if I hadn't."

"Oh, you're embroiled whether you want to be or not, chickadee," grunted Gran.

"Did you see anyone else when you were at the library?" asked Odelia.

"Well, I saw Malcolm Buckerfield," said Rockwell. "Ackerman's publisher? I told him I couldn't go through with the reading and he said he understood. Then again, he wasn't Ackerman's publisher anymore. Chris dumped him and negotiated a new deal with Franklin Cooper. Very lucrative, too, or so I heard."

"What was Buckerfield doing there?" asked Odelia.

"Probably trying to convince Chris to stay with him. Malcolm was desperate. Ackerman was his biggest author. Losing him would mean losing a big chunk of change."

"Would it be accurate to assume that losing Ackerman meant losing the business?"

Rockwell thought about that for a moment. "I doubt it. For one thing, Chris's entire backlist stays with Buckerfield Publishing, and those books will continue to sell. So to answer your question, losing Chris was a big blow, but it wouldn't have jeopardized the business."

"But don't you agree that Chris Ackerman's death benefits Mr. Buckerfield greatly? That backlist will be worth even more now."

"That's true," Rockwell acknowledged. "Every time a writer dies the value of his backlist suddenly goes up. But that's only a short-term effect. Eventually people forget. New authors arrive on the scene and the old guard is forgotten. Who remembers Harold Robbins or Sidney Sheldon or Arthur Hailey? Those guys were million-sellers. So unless the publisher hires a ghostwriter, like in Robert Ludlum's case, and continues to churn out the more lucrative block-buster series into perpetuity, those sales are going to dwindle and die."

"Chris Ackerman never signed that deal with Franklin Cooper," said Odelia. "Which means he's still a Buckerfield author, and new books will be published by his old publisher."

It was obvious from the expression on her face that she was thinking hard. This was obviously a new line of inquiry. And a most interesting one at that.

"If you put it that way," Rockwell admitted, "Malcolm had a lot to gain from Chris's death. Though any deal he wants to make will have to be made with Chris's heirs."

"Angelique and Trey Ackerman," said Odelia slowly.

Yup. The plot was definitely thickening. Like molasses.

The conversation continued for a while, and I actually started to nod off. In my defense, it had been a long night and half a day, and as everyone knows cats need their eighteen hours of sleep if they're going to function at maximum capacity. I'd just started dreaming of some nice Cat Snax when all of a sudden a sharp yapping sound woke me up.

When I searched around for the source of the noise, my eyes finally settled on a tiny dog. In fact it was the tiniest dog I'd ever seen, no bigger than a teacup. Which made Rockwell Burke's next comment very apt indeed.

"Don't mind her. That's Paris, my teacup Yorkie. She's adorable, isn't she?"

Adorable was not the word that sprang to mind at the sight of the lilliputian long-haired mutt. The thing kept barking furiously, so finally I decided to take matters in hand by shouting, "Hey! What's the matter with you?"

This seemed to startle the dog to the extent that it gave two more halfhearted yaps then shut up and sat staring at us, its little pink tongue lolling.

"We better have a chat with her," said Dooley. "That's what we're here for, right?"

Dooley was right. And even though having a chat with a miniature dog was the last thing I wanted to do, I dragged my weary body from the floor and strode towards the window, which had been opened a crack.

"You," I told the dog, not in the mood to mince my words, "come here."

And lo and behold. Paris, the teacup Yorkie, came there.

CHAPTER 24

"Who are you guys?" she asked the moment we'd set paw out on the balcony.

"My name is Dooley," said Dooley, enunciating slowly, as if talking to a toddler. Or a dog. "And this is Max. We're here to ask you some questions about your human. First question. Are you a living dog or an undead one? Think hard before you respond, dog."

"My name is Paris, and of course I'm not an undead dog. Why would you even ask such a stupid question?"

Dooley appeared taken aback by all this backtalk. "All right, all right," he muttered. "Don't bite my head off. I was just asking you a perfectly intelligent question."

"An undead dog! There's no such thing."

"Second question," said Dooley. "Have you always been such a tiny fuzzball?"

For a moment I was afraid Paris would blow her top. Instead, she snarled at Dooley for a moment, bearing surprisingly sharp teeth. Dooley immediately jerked back to a safe position well out of toothshot or even scratchshot. I didn't blame him. Then again, it's not very gentlemenlike to call a lady a tiny fuzzball. I wouldn't like it either. I'll bet not even Lassie, notoriously a very kind and sweet dog, would let such a slur slide without payback.

"Forgive my friend," I said, deciding to strike the conciliatory note. "He's an idiot."

"He sure is," said Paris, still glaring at Dooley.

"The thing is, someone killed a writer last night, and seeing as your human is also a writer, we figured we'd better get to the bottom of this thing fast, before it spreads."

I let that sink in for a moment. Finally, she got it. "You mean there's a serial killer on the loose who targets writers? That's horrible! That's dreadful! How many has he killed?"

"One, but you never know how fast a thing like that spreads."

Paris looked appropriately concerned. "I mean, Rockwell was supposed to meet this Ackerman fellow last night."

"You were there?"

"Of course I was. Rockwell doesn't go anywhere without me. I was tucked away in his man purse as usual, my head sticking out, and we hadn't even entered the library before he seemed to change his mind and walked out again."

"Just like that."

"Just like that. He muttered something to himself about not being a sellout and that was that. He got back into his rental and drove back to the hotel. He spent the rest of the evening in the hotel bar getting seriously plastered before coming up here and passing out."

"So he never met Ackerman?"

"He met a fat man—a publisher. Which suited me just fine. I heard Ackerman liked Rottweilers. I don't like Rottweilers. Rottweilers eat dogs like me for breakfast."

"I don't like Rottweilers either," said Dooley from behind a wicker patio chair.

Paris ignored him. "So are you any closer to catching this killer? I like my human. I don't want him to die."

"None of us want our humans to die," I said reassuringly. "And Odelia's uncle does have a man in custody who may or may not have killed Chris Ackerman. It's just that it's very hard to be sure."

"Why? Just use thumbscrews on the guy. I can guarantee a confession."

Obviously Paris belonged to the Vesta Muffin school of thought. I grimaced. "That would be a violation of his human rights," I said.

"What about my rights? If I lose my human I'll be homeless."

"Don't worry, Paris," said Dooley. "We'll catch this guy."

Paris tilted her chin and held up her paw. "Talk to the paw, cat."

It was obvious there was nothing more to learn here. Which was just as well, as Odelia had appeared on the balcony, announcing that her interview was over, too.

"See ya, Paris," I said.

The Yorkie gave me a smoldering look I found hard to interpret. Once I was inside, though, she yelled, "Thumbscrews, cat! Use thumbscrews! Think about my animal rights!"

"A dog after my own heart," muttered Gran, and then we were on our merry way.

And not a moment too soon. I needed some food, a long nap, and a total absence of teacup piglets or miniature Yorkies. At least we could rule out Rockwell Burke as a suspect. If Paris said he didn't do it, he didn't do it. The tiny dog might be a handful—at least if that hand belonged to a person with very small hands—but she was definitely not a liar.

As we arrived in the lobby, we came upon a strange scene. This time no teacups were involved. What was involved was a disheveled-looking young man, dressed in ragged pants and a long-sleeved hooded sweatshirt, shouting obscenities at the receptionist, who was clearly not happy about being accosted like this.

"Sir, I have called the police and they will have you removed from the premises," the receptionist said. He stood a little stiffly, like a knight of old prepared to defend his lordship's castle against an invading marauder.

"And I'm telling you I have to see Ackerman!" the young man screamed, banging his fists on the counter.

"I'm afraid Mr. Ackerman is no longer with us," said the receptionist.

"I know he's here! You can't hide him from me—where is he? Ackerman! ACKERMAN!"

"Poor fella," said Gran. "He's obviously delusional." Before Odelia could stop her, she walked up to the young man. "Mr. Ackerman is dead, son," she said, loud enough to attract the raving lunatic's attention.

For a moment, he fixed his eyes on her, and I could tell from the way his pupils were dilated that he'd imbibed some type of illegal substance. "You're lying!" he told Gran. "He's not dead! Ackerman can't die! He's immortal!"

"Yeah, keep telling yourself that, buddy," said Gran.

The kid pounded his chest. "I'm immortal! I'll live forever! ACKERMAN! ACKERMAN! ACKERMAN!"

"Oh, give it a rest," said Gran, who didn't like people making a fuss.

At this, the kid suddenly turned on her. "You're evil, old woman—you're part of the conspiracy to keep me away from Ackerman!"

"Gran, watch out!" Odelia shouted.

The kid had pulled back his fist and was about to give Gran a good pounding. The old lady must have seen it coming, though, for she'd quickly dug into her purse, brought out a small can of indeterminable origin, and the next moment was spraying it straight at her attacker's face. I have no idea what it was, but it definitely made an impact.

"Aaaaaarrgggh!" he said, and dropped to the floor, clawing at his eyes.

Moments later, Chase Kingsley came hurrying through the lobby doors, accompanied by three more cops, and before long the troublemaker was duly booked and dragged off to prison, where hopefully he'd calm down a little.

"Who the heck was that?" asked Gran.

"Stalker," said Chase.

"Who was he stalking?" asked Gran.

"Ackerman," said Chase.

"That would explain the yelling and raving," said Odelia.

"He wasn't supposed to come within a hundred yards of Ackerman. Obviously he had math issues."

"Technically not," said Odelia. "Ackerman isn't here, so he wasn't in breach of his restraining order."

Chase rubbed his chin, thoughtful, then locked eyes with Odelia. "You don't think…"

"That he was at the library last night?"

Chase turned to Gran. "You were there, Mrs. Muffin. Is he one of the people you saw?"

"Um…" Gran darted a quick look down at us. Unfortunately Big Mac wasn't amongst those present, so all I could do was shrug. "Ooh!" suddenly said Gran, bringing a hand to her head. "Do I suddenly feel woozy! Must be delayed shock from being attacked by that crazy hooligan. I better take a seat." She walked off, giving me and Dooley a big wink.

"Check the sketches," said Odelia, and Chase duly took out his phone and did just that.

For a moment, he flicked through the seven sketches Lara Dun had made on Big Mac's instigation, then he growled, "Bingo." He looked up, an expression of triumph on his face. "It's him. He *was* at the library last night. And if his present behavior is any indication, there's a good chance he's the guy we've been looking for."

CHAPTER 25

hase was in his favorite position: seated next to his commanding officer, across the table from a known culprit, ready to sweat the guy until he confessed. Once again they were in the interview room of the police precinct, and this time the culprit in the hot seat was the 'crazy hooligan' who'd recently been maced by Grandma Muffin.

The shabby-looking man's eyes were still red-rimmed and teary, but he'd calmed down on the ride over, and even more after spending about an hour in solitary lockup.

"Darius Kassman," said Chase. "What were you doing at the Hampton Cove library last night, when you weren't supposed to be anywhere near Chris Ackerman?"

Darius, a white-haired youth with bad skin, gave Chase a baleful look. "You can't keep me away from Ackerman, dude. That man is like the sun and I'm the planet that revolves around him. He draws me in."

"Planets aren't drawn in by the sun. If that were the case they would be destroyed," Chief Alec pointed out.

"Exactly, man. Ackerman is destroying me. His brilliance is such that it's devouring me. Wiping me out."

"Please tell us what you were doing at the library," Chase repeated.

"Like I told you—Ackerman called me."

"Called you," said Alec dubiously. "Like, literally called you on your phone?"

Darius tapped his temple. "He called me in here, dude. He's been calling me for a long time. Telling me 'Come—come to me. Be with me. Be me.' It's been tough getting here —seeing as some cops picked me up in Philly two nights ago —but here I am. I heeded the call."

"You were arrested for the possession of illegal substances," said Chase. "And released on your own recognizance."

"The judge knew I had a higher purpose to fulfill," said Darius, nodding. "No prison could have kept me away from Ackerman and she knew it. So here I am." He spread his arms. "Tell Ackerman His Loyal Servant has come. I commend my soul to him—to do with as he sees fit."

"Mr. Ackerman was killed last night, Darius," said Chief Alec. "Did you kill him?"

Darius frowned briefly, then laughed. "You're trying to confuse me. Is this a test?"

"This is not a test. Mr. Ackerman is dead and we're trying to figure out who killed him. Was it you?"

But Darius had covered his ears and was shaking his head. "Ackerman, Ackerman, Ackerman," he was saying softly, swaying back and forth.

Chase sighed, and so did Alec. They both got up at the same time, and walked out. In the hallway, Alec said, "I don't think we're going to get a lot more out of him right now."

"He's not exactly of sound mind and body," Chase agreed.

"He is the second suspect I like, though. In fact I like him even more than Drood."

They pondered this for a moment. Like kids having to

pick and choose between Reese's Pieces Peanut Butter Cups or Reese's Stuffed Chocolate Chip Cookies, it was hard to determine which suspect was the better choice, the robber or the crazed stalker druggie. Finally, Alec said, "Let's keep him overnight. Have another crack at him in the morning."

And Chase said that this was a great idea.

s Odelia and Gran were on their way back from the Hampton Cove Star, Dooley and Max napping on the backseat, she got a call from her boss, Hampton Cove Gazette editor Dan Goory.

"Dan. Have I got a story for you," she said before he could speak.

"I don't doubt it," said the aged editor. "And here's another one: Chris Ackerman's son is giving a press conference in front of the library where his father was killed last night and I want you there to write up the report."

"Ackerman's son? I just saw him. He didn't mention a press conference."

"Get me a couple of quotes, Odelia. And take some pictures, will you? This story has legs, I can feel it in my legs." He disconnected and Odelia promptly performed a U-turn.

"Hey—where are you going?" asked Gran, shaken out of her perusal of the footage she'd filmed so far.

"To the library. Trey Ackerman is holding a press conference."

"Weird. He didn't say nothing about no press conference."

"He probably didn't think it worth mentioning."

"Make it quick. I feel a nap coming on." Gran darted a quick look in the rearview mirror. "Too bad I'm not a cat. Those catnaps are pretty convenient."

Ten minutes later Odelia parked her car across the road

from the library and got out. Max opened one eye but then closed it again when Odelia gave his fur a gentle stroke.

"Sleep, buddy. You deserve it," she said.

She and Gran crossed the street. "Huh," said Gran. "That don't look like Trey Ackerman to me."

And indeed it didn't. A young man was standing on the library steps, a few passersby listening intently, and he definitely wasn't Trey Ackerman.

"I didn't know Ackerman had a second son," said Gran.

"That's because he doesn't," said Odelia. "At least not according to Wikipedia."

"Don't believe Wikipedia. They get it wrong all the time," said Gran. "Like that time they wrote that *The Bold and the Beautiful* had been canceled. *The Bold and the Beautiful* will never be canceled. At least not if CBS doesn't want a minor revolution on their hands."

"… and I will fight to my dying breath for the right to call Chris my dad," Ackerman's son was saying. He was a handsome fellow, with wavy blond hair, nice blue eyes and those clean-cut All-American features women fawn over. He even had nice teeth—so nice in fact that Odelia's tongue surreptitiously slid over her own set of choppers.

"Nice gnashers," Gran remarked.

"A dentist's wet dream," Odelia agreed.

"Forget dentists. He's *my* wet dream."

Odelia thought it better not to head down that road. "So who is this guy?"

"Aren't you listening? He's Chris Ackerman's son."

"… Chris was a good man. A kind man. A phenomenal writer. And he had an affair with my mother twenty-three years ago that led to an unwanted pregnancy. And even though Chris was too proud to admit it, a DNA test will confirm that I am, in fact, his son."

"Oops," said Gran.

Oops was right. Especially considering the fact that satellite trucks from at least three different TV stations came careening down the street. Soon reporters, camera crews in tow, had joined the melee and were shouting questions at the young man.

He enjoyed the attention, for he bared his perfect teeth in a wide smile and then announced, "Yesterday my name was Aldo Wrenn. But today my name is Aldo Ackerman!"

"Aldo Wrenn," said Odelia. "Google him, Gran."

"You Google him. I'm busy."

Odelia glanced at her grandmother and saw that she was filming the whole thing. Then suddenly the old woman lowered her phone and narrowed her eyes. "Say, isn't that the final guy on those sketches of mine? The ones I channeled for Big Mac?"

Odelia brought out her phone and checked the sketches, flicking through them just like Chase had done before. "Well, I'll be damned," she said finally. "You're right. He was at the library last night."

"Bingo!" said Gran, making a pumping motion with her fist. "Senior Sleuth is on a roll, baby."

"I thought you were a desperate housewife?"

"I'm changing my MO. From now on I want to be known as Granny Dick."

"Um… You might want to rethink that, Gran."

"Why? I'm a granny and I'm a private dick."

Odelia bit back a few choice remarks. Instead, she said, "Let's talk to Ackerman's newest son. See what he says."

"On it!" Gran cried enthusiastically. TV crews jostled to interview Aldo Wrenn—or Ackerman—but Gran muscled her way through the throng. "Coming through!" she yelled. "Make way for Granny Dick and Grandgirl Dick!"

Odelia ground her teeth. At least Gran wasn't using her can of Mace on the reporters.

A few snickers and lurid comments later, she reconsidered.

Maybe Gran *should* use her can of Mace on the reporters.

$\mathcal{I}$ woke up from some type of hubbub or ruckus and opened one eye to take a peek at its source. Across the street, in the library's courtyard, some kind of scuffle had broken out between a bunch of people carrying microphones and cameras. At the heart of the scuffle I recognized Gran and Odelia, womanfully trying to force their way through the throng to a guy who looked like he could feature as the lead in a Disney Channel Original Movie.

"What's going on?" asked Dooley, rising up next to me.

"I'm not sure. Looks like Gran and Odelia are trying to pick a fight with Zac Efron and a bunch of reporters are attempting to stop them."

Dooley yawned and stretched. "Oh, look. It's Big Mac."

He was right. Waddling across the street was the fast-food-loving cat.

"Hey, Big Mac!" I shouted. "Over here."

When he saw us, he gave us a kindly nod of the head, and toddled over.

Odelia had cranked the window down and Dooley and I

leaned out like seasoned window-leaners, elbows propped up on the doorframe.

"Hey, buds," said Big Mac, greeting us like old pals.

"Hey, buddy. We keep bumping into each other."

"Big Mac loves to go to the library," said Dooley.

"Big Mac loves to check out the dumpster behind the library," Big Mac corrected him. "Because that dumpster is equidistant from the two best pizza parlors in Hampton Cove, which, according to my calculations, borne out by the facts, means this dumpster is a great place to dig up some grade-A pizza leftovers."

"Max taught us that pizza boxes are a very important clue," said Dooley, apropos of nothing. "Pizza boxes lead Aurora Teagarden to solve her mysteries. She sees a pizza box and she knows. It's a great trick." He was nodding intelligently. "Isn't that right, Max?"

I was going to explain to Dooley, not for the first time, that pizza boxes were only a clue in those particular circumstances in that particular mystery on that particular TV show but sometimes one gets tired of repeating oneself so instead I said, "We found almost all of the people you identified, Big Mac. Only one is still missing from the list."

"He's over there," said Big Mac, gesturing to the library. "That spiffy-looking dude on the steps? He was here last night. I would recognize him anywhere. He looks like Brad Pitt before he was Brad Pitt."

"How do you know what Brad Pitt looked like before he was Brad Pitt?" I asked.

"My human is a big fan of supermarket tabloids. He can't go through a checkout line without buying a stack of them. And they always have those unflattering 'before they were famous' photomontages. I love them. You should see what George Clooney looked like."

Dooley had been thinking hard. I could tell, for his

tongue was sticking out of his mouth. Finally he voiced the question that was bugging him. "Wasn't Brad Pitt always Brad Pitt? Or did he change his name?"

Big Mac decided to ignore this outburst. Instead, he raised a point of interest. "Have you found the pizza guy?"

"I don't think the pizza guy is a high priority." I explained how two people on Big Mac's list were now languishing in the Hampton Cove lockup, both competing for the dubious honor of being Chris Ackerman's killer, so his pizza delivery guy wasn't exactly on anyone's radar right now. I further argued that pizza guys don't go around killing their customers with expensive fountain pens. He agreed that there was something in that.

"Still," he said. "He didn't smell right."

"He was a pizza guy. He probably smelled like a pizza guy."

"That's the thing, see," said Big Mac. "He didn't."

"So what did he smell like?" I asked.

"Soap."

"Soap."

"Yeah, soap. Freshly washed and bathed."

"So he was a fastidious pizza guy. So what?"

"Pizza guys have to smell like pizza," he insisted.

He was obviously old-fashioned that way, so I decided not to argue the point. As I saw it a pizza guy could smell like soap if he wanted to. In fact it was preferable. Nobody likes his pizza delivery person to smell like old socks or stinky pits. Bad for business, if you see what I mean. You want the pizza person to project that wholesome, clean image.

The pizza discussion had gone right over Dooley's head, as his next words indicated. "If Brad Pitt wasn't Brad Pitt before he was Brad Pitt, then who was he?"

"Oh, Dooley," I said with a sigh.

Big Mac tapped the car door with his paw. "Gotta go,

fellas. People to see, pizza leftovers to gobble up. Catch you later, all right?"

"See ya, Big Mac," I said, and watched the big cat wobble across the road. Then I thought of something. "Hey, Big Mac?"

"Yo," said the big cat, turning.

"Wanna join cat choir? Tonight at the park. Practically all the cats of Hampton Cove will be there. We hang out, sing some tunes, shoot the breeze. What do you say?"

"I can't sing, dude."

"None of us can."

He shrugged. "I'll think about it." He held up a paw and I returned the gesture. As he walked away, he softly sang, "I'm lovin' it." Yep, he really did love it.

There was a momentary silence after Big Mac had left, then Dooley said, "So about Brad Pitt…"

CHAPTER 27

Odelia and Gran had a hard time getting Chris Ackerman's latest son to give them the time of day. As it was, he was giving exclusive interviews left and right, passing out quotes like candy. More media people were arriving by the busload—magically multiplying like Agent Smith in *The Matrix*—and suddenly the young man was the hottest thing in town.

And who could blame the media for converging on this latest sensational story? Chris Ackerman was, after all, a world-famous author, and his mysterious murder had only made him more famous. And now here was a son no one had ever heard about, turning Ackerman, who in all honesty had looked more like a stodgy old college professor than a Calvin Klein underwear model, into someone who sold magazines and invited those all-precious clicks.

Before long, the scene turned into something out of a Mel Gibson movie, with reporters hitting each other over the head with their microphones and pimpled, pasty-faced and overweight cameramen staring each other down, ready to rumble.

"Your colleagues are *nasty*," said Gran after a female reporter with nails like Rihanna had stomped on her toe. She was rooting around in her purse, presumably in search of her can of Mace, and Odelia quickly thought of ways and means to avert the impending disaster.

"They're not my colleagues," said Odelia. "A lot of these people are celebrity gossip bloggers, so they're more your colleagues than mine."

Gran took offense. "I'm nothing like them. I ply my trade with dignity and poise."

"Which is why you can't wait to mace them."

"It's all about the competitive edge, honey. This is a cutthroat business."

And if she didn't stop her grandmother, throats would definitely get cut.

At that moment, though, the whoop of a police siren sounded nearby, and soon cops were descending on the scene.

"We better get out of here," said Odelia. "Before the riot police starts busting heads and breaking bones."

"They better don't break my bones or I'll sue them for millions."

"Your son heads the police department!"

"Never let sentiment muddle your thinking, honey. I saw that on *Mary Poppins*."

They both moved to the side, and watched as Uncle Alec's troops returned order to the mob scene. Chase spotted them on the edge of the crowd, and sauntered over.

"What's this I hear about some dude telling people he's Chris Ackerman's son?"

"Better ask him yourself," said Gran. "We tried to interview him but there was no getting through those nasty reporters. Oh, and before you ask, he's one of the people I identified this morning. You'll find his sketch in your files."

"His name is Aldo Wrenn," said Odelia. "Only now he calls himself Aldo Ackerman."

"Whenever a celebrity dies there's always a rash of these bogus claims," said Chase. "Remember when Prince died? Over seven hundred people claimed to be his siblings."

"I could have been Prince's sister," said Gran. "What?" she added when Odelia gave her a piercing look. "I'm not saying I *am* his sister. Just saying I *could* have been."

"What makes you think you and Prince were related?" asked Chase, genuinely curious.

Promptly Gran lifted the leg of her colorful track pants to display a bony white calf. "Just look at my legs."

Chase looked at Gran's leg. "N-nice," he said in a slightly choked voice.

"I should think so. These are some princely legs. I'll bet Prince's sister has legs just like these and so does his momma. And then of course I've got a voice just like Prince."

"You do?" asked Chase.

"You don't have to be beautiful. To turn me on," the old lady began to sing in a reedy voice. It sounded nothing like Prince, but she was shaking that leg, and batting her eyelashes like a pro. A pro pole dancer, though, not a pro singer.

Chase suppressed a smile. "That's pretty awesome, Mrs. Muffin," he said finally.

"Just call me Vesta. I think it's time we got on a first-name basis," she cooed, placing a hand on Chase's bicep while she recuperated from her impromptu dance routine.

Chase had the good decency to blush. "Yes, ma'am," he said.

Uncle Alec walked over, and Odelia was happy to see he came bearing gifts in the form of Aldo Wrenn—or Ackerman. The moment she and Gran had discovered Aldo was the seventh person Big Mac had identified, she'd shot off a message to her uncle. And a good thing, too, considering Aldo's impromptu press conference had almost gotten out of hand.

"I think we better hold this conversation at the station, son," said Alec.

"Why? What did I do?" asked Aldo.

"First off, you managed to disturb the peace. Second…" He nodded to Odelia. "You were seen at this here library last night, just before Chris Ackerman was killed. So I'm gonna want a statement from you about that."

"That wasn't me! I swear!"

CHAPTER 28

"Yeah, that was me," said Aldo, sounding a lot less cocky than before. Then again, being dragged into a police station instead of *CBS This Morning* will do that to a person.

Odelia watched on from the next room.

"I'm having déjà vu," said Gran. "It feels like we've been here before."

"We've been here before," said Odelia.

"How do people do this? Sit in that tiny room all day talking to dirtbags?"

"We don't know if he's a dirtbag yet."

"He looks like a dirtbag."

"With nice teeth."

"With great teeth."

"So why were you at the library last night?" asked Uncle Alec. Next to him, Chase was drumming his fingers on the table, scrutinizing this new addition to Chris Ackerman's family.

"Look, I just wanted to talk to him, all right? I mean, can

you blame me? I just found out he was my dad. I wanted to get to know the guy. Create a bond, you know."

"You mean, go fishing together? Watch a ball game?"

"Yeah! Exactly!"

"So why does Angelique Ackerman swear up and down you're not Chris's son?"

"Of course she would say that. Especially now that my father is dead and she stands to inherit."

"You know what I find weird about this?" said Chase. "That you waited to come forward until now. The day after your alleged father died. Doesn't that strike you as odd, Chief?"

"It strikes me as extremely suspicious is what it strikes me as," Alec agreed.

"I tried to get in touch with Chris before yesterday. In fact I tried to get in touch with him many times. He stonewalled me. Only wanted to connect through his lawyers. So I did. I patiently laid down the facts again and again. How Chris had an affair with my mom twenty-three years ago. How nine months later I was born. How my mom swears Chris was the father but never told me before because Chris had broken her heart and she didn't want anything to do with him. And how she finally decided to come forward last year, when she was diagnosed with cancer and told she only had months to live."

"So how is your mother now?" asked Uncle Alec.

"She's fine. In remission."

Chase was shaking his head and smiling. He obviously didn't buy it.

"It's all true!" cried Aldo. "Ask her. She'll confirm everything. The affair, the pregnancy, the whole thing." He leaned in. "Look, all I wanted was to meet my dad."

"And did you? Meet him?"

Aldo looked away. "Yes, I did."

"And? What did he say?"

"He said to get the hell out of there and never show my face again." He clenched his jaw. "He said a lot of other stuff that I won't repeat here. Suffice it to say it didn't go well."

"So you flew into a rage and plunged his fountain pen into his neck," Chase supplied.

"No! Of course not. Why would I kill my own father? I told him I'd give him some time to think about it and I'd be in touch. He said that if I ever approached him again he'd get a restraining order. So I just left. But…"

"But what?" asked Uncle Alec.

"I did something I probably shouldn't have."

"You killed him."

"No! How many times do I have to say it? I didn't kill my father. I grabbed a hair from his cardigan and tucked it into my pocket. Then when I got to the hotel I put it in a plastic baggie and now I'm having it tested against one of my own for a DNA match." He tapped the table with his finger. "Chris Ackerman was my father and I'm going to prove it."

"Nasty business," commented Gran.

"Angelique isn't going to like it," Odelia said.

"She's going to blow her top is what she's going to do."

Odelia thought Gran was right. Just now that Angelique stood to inherit a nice chunk of change here came this kid who, if he was right, could throw a big wrench in the works.

"Do you think he's our killer?" she asked.

"Nah. He looks too cute to be a killer."

"I thought you said he looks like a dirtbag?"

"I changed my mind. I think he's the real deal."

Odelia had that impression as well. Still, it was plenty suspicious that Aldo would show up today and not sooner. Almost as if he'd been waiting for his father to die. Unless he was his father's killer, and now he was here to claim his prize. Like in *Game of Thrones*, where chopping off a king's head and then snatching his throne was the fashion du jour.

Not that Aldo had chopped off his father's head. He may have made a start, though, by plunging in that pen.

"This case is getting more complicated by the minute. So many suspects!"

"Don't complain. It's better to have too many suspects than not enough."

"But how do we know who did it?"

"Intuition, honey," said Gran. "A real dick knows."

"I really wish you wouldn't use that word, Gran."

"What, dick? What's wrong with calling a spade a spade? I'm a private dick and so are you. We're dicks together. Now if you could drive me home my shows are about to start and you know I can't miss those, dick or no dick."

CHAPTER 29

*T*ex Poole had just seen his last patient of the day and blew out a sigh of relief. It had been a long day, and he wasn't feeling at his best after a long and sleepless night. First his wife's Author of the Month evening had gone so horribly, terribly wrong, then they'd had to stick around while the police did their thing, and then once they'd arrived home Marge had been in no fit state to go to bed so they'd stayed up talking and sipping cups of chamomile tea, which was supposed to work wonders on a strained nervous system.

He'd have preferred to give his wife a Xanax or a Valium. Or a Klonopin or an Ativan. Or maybe something a little stronger. But Marge wasn't one for popping pills. She preferred a more naturalistic approach. She believed in homeopathy, Bach Flower Remedies and aromatherapy. Every morning she did her yoga exercises, and from time to time she visited a reflexologist, a shiatsu guy and an acupuncturist. She'd recently even taken up mindfulness.

All in all, she was a doctor's worst nightmare. Then again, she was also his wife, and he loved her, so whatever she did was just fine by him. As long as it didn't endanger her health or her overall wellbeing, which of course these placebo methods wouldn't.

And Tex had just gotten up from his desk and picked his jacket from the coatrack in the corner of his office when a knock on the door surprised him. He'd had to make do today without Grandma Muffin at the receptionist's desk. The old lady had gotten it into her head that she wanted to become a detective and her first case was Chris Ackerman's murder.

Tex strode over to the door and opened it. To his even greater surprise he found Chase Kingsley standing on the mat. The stalwart detective eyed him apologetically.

"Tex," he said. "I hope I'm not intruding. I saw there were no patients so I figured…"

"Yeah, no, come on in, Chase," said Tex, jovially clapping the other man on the back. "So what can I do for you?" he asked once they were both seated. "Something ailing you?"

"Physically I'm in fine fettle," said Chase surprisingly. "It's actually your daughter I wanted to talk to you about."

Tex drew both eyebrows up into his white fringe. A man with a great head of hair, he was the epitome of the country doctor. Hale and hearty and bluff, he was both kindly and knowledgeable. On top of that he genuinely liked his fellow man and woman and was always ready to do his little bit to improve their lot in life—be it medically or otherwise.

Chase's response threw him for a loop, though. He'd always viewed Chase as the perfect son-in-law and the perfect mate for his daughter. In fact he'd been thanking his lucky stars on a daily basis ever since Chase had entered their lives. And now this?

"Odelia? Is there something wrong with my daughter, Chase?"

"Oh, no. Nothing is wrong, sir. Nothing at all. It's just that…" Chase rubbed his square jaw, looking sheepish. "The thing is..." He cleared his throat. "The fact of the matter is, sir..."

"Oh, please cut the 'sir' thing, son. We've known each other long enough now for you to call me by my Christian name."

"Yes, Tex," said Chase dutifully.

Tex waited patiently. He'd had patients who were so reluctant to talk about their ailments that it took him almost the entire allotted time to drag it out of them. Chase looked like he was going to need even more than that. "So? Just spit it out, son," he said finally when no more information seemed forthcoming.

Chase steeled himself. "I'm just going to come out and say it, sir—Tex. The thing is, I like your daughter a lot... Tex. In fact I love her. Love her a whole damn lot. And what I wanted to ask you, sir, is this..." He cleared his throat noisily. If he'd had a hat, he would have turned it over nervously between his fidgety fingers.

Oh, darn it, Tex thought. This was it, wasn't it? This was that scene you saw in the movies. Where the future son-in-law asked his future father-in-law for the hand of his daughter in marriage. The fresh-faced freckled youth would preface his remarks with a few well-meant 'gee whizes' and 'oh, gollys' and pepper them with a few 'aw, shucks' when finally his future dad-in-law gave his blessing. At which point cigars would be brought out and both men would smoke a fat gasper while gazing fondly off into the horizon.

Tex rearranged his avuncular face into an expression of solemnity befitting the occasion. "Ye-es," he said slowly, knitting his fingers on his desk's blotter.

"The thing is, sir—Tex..." Chase halted, then started again. "The thing is that Odelia and I were moving in a direction I thought... And then her grandmother moved in and..."

Tex nodded. He knew exactly where Chase was coming

from. Marge's mother had been the bane of his existence for many, many years. In fact she was the one person who sometimes made him doubt his calling as a man devoted to stop people from dying.

"And now I don't know how to proceed," Chase said, lifting his arms in a gesture of confusion.

Tex finally saw all. This man hadn't come here to ask for his blessing. He'd come to seek some fatherly advice on how to woo Odelia. Grandma Muffin's shenanigans had torn these two lovebirds asunder and now it was up to Tex to put them together again. Chase's dad had died years ago, so he had no other father figure to turn to other than Tex. And Tex was happy to take on the role—in fact he was honored—even touched to the verge of tears.

"Chase," he said in his warmest, most gregarious manner, "I'm going to let you in on a little secret."

Chase shifted forward on his chair. He looked eager. "Yes, sir—I mean, Tex?"

"This secret has the power to unlock the heart of any Poole woman." Except Vesta, but that was because she was a Muffin, not a Poole. And because she didn't have a heart.

"Yes?" said Chase, hanging on Tex's every word now.

"This is the method I used to woo and win Odelia's mother's heart, and this is the method you, if you choose to accept the mission, can use to win over my little girl's heart."

He choked back a tear. A sudden image of Odelia dressed in white striding down the aisle on his arm had suddenly flashed through his mind. "This is what you need to do."

Chase was practically falling from his chair, his ears pricked up, his eyes wide.

"One word," said Tex. "Serenade."

Chase stared at Tex. Tex smiled at Chase. When the cop didn't speak, Tex threw his arms wide. "You have to serenade her, son! Go old school. Head on over to Odelia's house at the stroke of midnight, take up your position under the balcony, and belt out your finest ballad. I'd suggest Frankie Avalon's *Venus*. Worked like a charm for me. Marge loved it."

Grandma Muffin had loved it a lot less. Marge had still been living at home at the time, and Tex had gotten mixed up about whose window he was under. Gran had poured out her chamber pot on top of Tex's head, later claiming she'd figured he was a cat in heat.

Which of course he was.

"A ballad," said Chase dubiously.

"A ballad," said Tex, smiling winsomely.

"There's only one problem, Tex. I can't sing."

"Neither can I, but that didn't stop me. Look, son. If you're going to win my daughter's heart, you're going to have to make a bold move. Trust me, women love men who make bold moves."

"Do they also love men who make total, utter fools of themselves?"

"They do, they do," said Tex, though he kinda doubted it. "I'm sure you won't make a fool of yourself, though. Sing."

"What?"

"Sing. Pick any song and let me hear what you're capable of. Judging from your speaking voice I'm pretty sure you've got a nice baritone. Women love a nice baritone."

When Chase didn't make any attempt to burst into song, Tex switched on the small radio that was located next to his desk. As luck would have it, the unforgettable Sam Cooke was singing.

"Try it," said Tex kindly. "Sing along with the maestro."

Hesitantly, Chase yowled, *"She was only sixteen, only sixteen..."*

"Mh," said Tex, folding his hands in front of his face and tucking in his chin. "Let's pick another one. Odelia is not sixteen, after all."

"What about my voice?" asked Chase eagerly. "Do you think it holds up?"

Tex decided not to go there. Your kindly music teacher knows when to refrain from criticism and turn up the encouragement instead. He changed channels on his small radio and Neil Sedaka's voice filled the room.

Dutifully, Chase sang, *"Oh! Carol, I am but a fool."*

"Nice," Tex coached. "Try to focus on the melody. Yes, that's it."

"If you leave me I will surely die," Chase warbled, switching from his impersonation of an asthmatic sheep to that of Walter the singing French Bulldog.

Tex winced, though he tried not to show it. It was clear that Chase would never get past the first auditions for *The Voice* or *American Idol*. "That's great, Chase," he said finally, clapping his hands encouragingly. "I've heard enough." That, and his ears were bleeding.

Chase gave him an expectant look. "Do you think I've got what it takes, Doc?"

"Oh, sure, sure," said Tex. "Odelia will love it. Love it!" More likely she'd take pity on the poor sap and kiss him to end the torture, both his and hers. He smiled at the tough cop. "Though you might want to choose a different song. Something more attuned to my daughter's musical sensibilities."

"She likes Ed Sheeran," said Chase with enthusiasm.

"There you go," said Tex, who had no idea who Ed Sheeran was.

"Perfect," said Chase.

"Well, you know what they say about perfection. It doesn't exist."

"No, *Perfect* is the name of the song."

"Oh, swell." And as they walked out of the office, Tex reminded himself to buy a new pair of earplugs.

CHAPTER 30

That night, Dooley, Brutus and I headed into town with a very specific mission in mind: we were going to save Brutus utilizing the power vested in Shanille by a higher being.

Frankly I had my doubts whether Shanille had any power vested in her other than the power to lead cat choir, but Brutus's mind was made up and we'd promised him to stand by his side and hold his paw if need be.

We were looking up at the large oak front doors of St. John's Church, which is where Shanille's human Father Reilly works. I have no idea what denomination he belongs to. Humans seem to have so many churches to choose from it frankly boggles the mind. All I knew was that somewhere inside this building salvation awaited. At least in Brutus's mind.

"Let's get this over with," I said, and proceeded up the stone steps.

The doors to Shanille's church are always open, which is kinda neat in this day and age of the ubiquitous burglar or thieving scoundrel. Then again, who would steal from a church? Instant karma probably hits you with a lightning bolt the moment you try. Or is it the god of the humans who takes care of that? As you can tell I'm a little fuzzy on the details.

I had to push hard to gain entrance to the church, but Dooley and Brutus were there to give me a helping paw. Together we managed, the door slowly easing closed again behind us. The church was pretty dark, but I didn't mind. I could see plenty. The ceiling was high above us, and tall pillars stood in support of the large structure. Rows of wooden pews had been placed facing an altar, and every-where I looked I could see statues of humans dressed in some pretty funky outfits. My best guess was that they were either hippies or that they'd lived a really long time ago. At some point I thought I saw a statue of a sheep, but my eyes were probably deceiving me. No human would worship a sheep. Now if it had been a cat…

"Over here," suddenly a voice rang out. It sounded hollow and echoed through the large cavernous structure. I recog-nized it as belonging to Shanille so we trotted thither.

"This place is seriously spooky," I ventured.

"This is a holy place, Max," Brutus said. "It can't be spooky."

Yes, it could, and it was.

We padded across the granite floor, pews to the left of us and pews to the right, until we reached the front—or was it the back? There Shanille awaited us, looking solemn.

"I thought you wouldn't show," she said.

"Wouldn't miss it for the world," I muttered.

"My spots have become worse," Brutus revealed, and thrust out his chest, parting his perm with his paws. I looked and he was right. More spots. Yikes. Involuntarily I took a step back, and so did Dooley. Shanille, the only professional healer present, took a step closer and put her paw on Brutus's shoulder, fixing him with a kindly gaze.

"Before the night is through, you will be healed, Brutus," she announced.

"Gee, thanks," said Brutus. "That's exactly what I needed to hear." He then gave me and Dooley a dirty look. "You two knuckleheads said you were going to hold my paw."

"Yeah, well, maybe Shanille should do the honors," I said. "She's done this before, after all." When Shanille looked away, I added, "You *have* done this before, right?"

"Um... not technically," she admitted. And when I rolled my eyes, she said, "I've done it to myself."

"You baptized yourself."

"Well, I had to. It's not as if I could ask my human. 'Please, Francis, could you baptize me?' That would have gone over well. Besides, unlike Odelia he doesn't speak feline so my paws were tied."

"Wait, Father Reilly's name is Francis?" I asked.

But she was already walking away towards a large stone basin located behind the altar to the right. This was where humans baptized their babies. They pour water over their little heads and that's it. No idea why but then who knows why humans do anything.

"Come," ordered Shanille.

Brutus took a deep breath. "This is it, Max," he said.

"This is it, buddy," I agreed.

And then he took the plunge. Not literally. But he set one paw in front of the other and pretty soon we were all staring at Shanille, hoping she knew what she was doing. The thing is, cats don't like water. At least not in general. So us willingly and consciously having water splashed on top of our heads was kind of a crazy thing to do. Then again, if I had to choose between horrible spots and a bath, I'd choose the bath. Lesser of two evils, right?

"Hop up," instructed Shanille, and in an effort to lead by example, she hopped up onto the baptismal font herself, followed by Dooley, Brutus and, finally, yours truly.

The inside of the font was dark, the stone having turned black over the years. We stared into the water, and for a moment I imagined staring into an abyss. Creepy!

"Who wants to go first?" asked Shanille.

"Me, me, me!" said Dooley, holding up his paw.

"Very well," said Shanille. "Um…" She hesitated.

"What's wrong?" asked Dooley.

"The thing is, Father Reilly always says a lot of stuff at this point, but I'm always too far away to hear a word he says. Plus, he kinda mumbles a lot, so there's that, too."

"He does mumble," I agreed.

"So I have no idea what he says but he looks very serious and solemn while he says it. And I'm pretty sure it's something to do with Jesus, the Holy Ghost, and the Father."

"Whose father?" asked Dooley, interested.

"Father Reilly's father," I said. "Duh."

"Pretty sure he means God," said Shanille.

"Oh."

"Yeah."

"So what I propose is that I say a few words of my own creation and then proceed like I've seen Father Reilly do. Which basically is to splash some water on y'all."

I grimaced. "Sounds like a plan," I said.

"Let's get on with it," Brutus growled. "I can feel my spots getting bigger by the second."

"Fine," said Shanille. "Dooley, in the name of the—"

"Stop!" suddenly a voice echoed through the church. "Stop this abomination right now!"

When we turned we saw that none other than Harriet had joined us, and she didn't look happy.

CHAPTER 31

"*W*hat do you think you're doing?" Harriet demanded as she bore down on us.

"Getting baptized?" said Brutus, looking distinctly uneasy.

"Getting baptized my ass. You're getting married, aren't you?" She pointed an accusing finger at Shanille. "You're getting secretly married to that female feline!"

"No!" said Shanille shocked. "You're wrong, Harriet."

"Sneaking behind my back for your secret wedding. You should be ashamed of yourselves. You, too, Max. I can't believe you would agree to be a party to this nonsense."

"What about me?" asked Dooley.

"Of all the double-crossing, sneaky, devious, underhanded..." Harriet fumed.

"We're not getting married!" Brutus interrupted her harangue. "I mean, who has even heard of cats getting married? That's just nuts. And very human!"

Harriet narrowed her eyes at him. She looked absolutely terrifying right now, a regular queen of vengeance. "So what is this? A nice little get-together? Conveniently without inviting me? I don't think so. I hate you, Brutus. And you, Max."

"And me?" asked Dooley hopefully.

"And you, Shanille—I can't believe you would stab a fellow female feline in the back like that. Us females should stick together, not let these treacherous tomcats divide us."

"Can you shut up for one second?" Brutus suddenly roared, and he gave Harriet a look of such vexation that the latter closed her mouth with a click of the teeth. "I didn't want to tell you this but you leave me no choice. I'm dying, Harriet."

"Yes, you are," Harriet said.

"No, for real."

"I know. You're dead to me."

"I have spots!" Brutus cried out, desperation in his voice.

Whatever Harriet had been expecting, it wasn't this. She stared at Brutus. "Spots?"

"Spots! Red spots! On my chest!"

For a moment, Harriet was speechless. "Huh."

"So I asked Shanille for advice and she said inviting Jesus into my life would fix me right up."

"Jesus," said Harriet dubiously.

"Yes, Jesus. I'm a desperate cat, Harriet, and I didn't know what else to do."

"So why didn't you tell me?"

"I didn't want you to worry. Also…" He traced an uncertain pattern on the baptismal font's ledge with his paw. "I, um, I guess I felt embarrassed."

"Embarrassed!"

"I know you like your tomcats butch and strong, and these spots have made me feel weak and… well, all too aware of my own mortality. I didn't want to let you down."

"Oh, Brutus," she said, and to my elation there was a marked softening in her demeanor. In the past her 'Oh,

Brutus' had alternately sounded exasperated or incensed but now her words were tinged with a nice sense of compassion.

Brutus jumped down from the font and approached her. "I'm sorry," he said. "I should have told you. I didn't think I could stand to see the disappointment on your face."

"Disappointment! Brutus, I'm not disappointed. In fact I'm proud of you. That you would decide to face this terrible disease on your own—proud in the face of certain death."

There was a moment of reconciliation that was accompanied by the kind of scene that would almost certainly earn this chronicle a PG-13 rating so I won't recount it here. Suffice it to say that all seemed to be well in the enduring love affair of Harriet and Brutus.

"So are we still doing this?" asked Shanille, sounding a little peeved. A staunch believer in the life celibate, she hadn't enjoyed being accused of being married to Brutus.

"Yes, we're doing this," said Harriet with a happy smile. "In fact, now that I come to think of it, I want to join you guys. I want to invite Jesus into my life, too. Max, Brutus, I want to be baptized, too, if that's all right with you."

"What about me?!" Dooley cried.

Harriet gave him a grin. "Just teasing." She gestured between them. "I see you."

"Avatar!" Dooley jubilated. "I love that movie!"

"What's he talking about?" grumbled Brutus. For a cat on the verge of death he was no stranger to petty jealousy.

"Never mind," said Harriet, jumping up onto the baptismal font. "So how does this work?"

"Shanille will say a few words, then splash some water on our heads," I explained.

"Great. So let's get on with it. This cold stone is murder on my butt."

It wasn't exactly the kind of statement to preface what Shanille had said was the most important moment of our lives. I wasn't convinced she was right. The most important moment in my life had probably been when Odelia lifted me from amongst my mother's litter. The second most important moment when Dooley came into my life. But I wasn't about to be nitpicky. After all, this wasn't about me but about the salvation of Brutus.

Brutus joined us and now five cats circled the dark well of holy water.

"Let's begin," said Shanille. "Brutus, do you reject sin and the glamour of anvil?"

"Anvil?" I asked.

"That's what Father Reilly says on these occasions."

"Pretty sure he means 'evil.'"

"Are you a church cat or am I?"

"You are."

"Fine. Brutus, what say you?"

"Um, I reject the glamour of anvil," said Brutus.

"Max," whispered Dooley.

"What?"

"I thought I was first!"

"Let's just go with it," I suggested. Otherwise we'd be there all night. And Harriet was right. This cold bluestone surface was wreaking havoc on my tender tush.

"Do you believe in the Holy Sprite?" Shanille intoned.

"Spirit," I muttered.

Shanille gave me a withering look and I mimicked locking my lips and throwing away the key.

"Sure thing, babe," said Brutus with a grin. Like Big Mac, he was clearly lovin' it.

"And do you believe in Jesus Christ, our Lord and Savior?"

"Absolutely, toots," said Brutus, earning himself a scowl from Shanille.

"Brutus, I now baptize you in the name of the Father, the

Son and the Holy Sprite, for the forgiveness of your sins, and the gift of the Holy Sprite."

"So what about my spots?" asked Brutus.

In response, a clearly irate Shanille gave Brutus a slap on the back that sent the black cat flying into the baptismal font. When he resurfaced, spluttering and splashing, she made the sign of the cross and said, "Consider yourself baptized. Next!"

Dooley, Harriet and I exchanged worried glances. I'd expected a slight splash of water, which was enough to give me chills. But a full-body dunking? No way, José!

"Your turn," said Brutus, who now looked like a drowned chicken. He sneezed. "Hey, I feel better already." He quickly checked his spots. "Nah. They're still there."

"The benediction might take some time to kick in," Shanille said. "So who's next?"

Finally, Harriet stepped to the fore—metaphorically, at least—and said, with a slight shiver of anticipation, "Me. I wanna go next."

"Fine," said Shanille. "Harriet, do you reject sin and the glamour of anvil?"

And so it went. Harriet went into the drink, then Dooley, and finally, I was for it, too. I have to say that when all was said and done, I felt distinctly refreshed. Which of course could have had something to do with the fact that the water was pretty darn chilly.

Still, now that I'd put my destiny in the Lord Jesus's hands, I had the impression that this benediction Shanille had mentioned had descended upon my furry shoulders, too. It was the weirdest thing. As the four of us walked out of that church, it was with a spring in our collective steps, smiles on our faces and a definite swing in our hips.

"I can't believe we'll never have to go to Vena anymore," said Dooley, voicing my thoughts exactly.

"We'll never get sick again," said Harriet.

"And we'll never have to get shots ever again!" I cried.

We all laughed. If there's one thing us cats hate, it's shots.

Brutus sneezed, and then, like a chain reaction, so did Dooley, Harriet and me.

Looked like the Lord Jesus had washed away our sins and given us a cold in return.

CHAPTER 32

*W*hen Odelia woke up the next day she wondered for a moment what had awakened her. It wasn't her alarm—she'd forgotten to set it again—and it wasn't the sun shining through the curtains either, for the sun hadn't yet hoisted itself across the horizon yet.

"Achoo!"

She lifted her head from the pillow and saw, in the relative darkness of the room, a small form at the foot of the bed. She smiled and propped herself up on her elbows.

"Max? Is that you sneezing?"

In response, four distinctly different sneezes rang out like cannon shots in the silence of the room.

"Achoo!"

"Achee!"

"Achoum!"

"Achaa!"

She flicked on her bedside Betty Boop lamp and blinked against the sudden light. When her vision cleared, she saw four cats staring back at her. Max, Dooley, Harriet and

Brutus. They didn't look very happy. In fact they looked distinctly despondent.

"You have a cold," she said matter-of-factly. "All four of you."

All four cats nodded gloomily.

"I better take you to Vena," she said.

Four equally cheerless nods, followed by four more sneezes.

"Better tell her about your spots," said Max.

"Oh, all right," muttered Brutus.

"What spots?" asked Odelia.

"I have spots on my chest," Brutus announced. "They're red."

"Which is why we now all have a cold," explained Max.

"I don't get it," said Odelia. "How do you go from spots to a cold?"

"It's a long story," said Max. "And it involves a baptismal font with very cold water."

"It's all Shanille's fault," said Harriet. "I should have known that flighty feline would get us into trouble."

"At least our souls are with Jesus now," said Dooley.

Odelia blinked. Looked like it had been a long night for her cats. Checking her phone she saw that it wasn't even five o'clock yet. Pretty sure she wasn't going to be able to get back to sleep, she decided to get up instead. Moving over to the window, she peeked through the curtains and saw that first light was painting the sky in brilliant reds and blues.

"Can you guys give me a hand or are you too sick to do a little sleuthing?" she asked.

"I'm never too sick to do a little sleuthing," said Max.

"Great. I saw this on a TV show the other day. It's called a vision board."

She tripped down the stairs, four cats close on her heels, switched on the lights in her cozy little living room and gestured triumphantly to the whiteboard the UPS guy had delivered the day before. "Ta-dah!" she said.

"*Achoo!*" said Max in earnest admiration.

"What is it?" asked Dooley.

"A vision board," said Max.

"Yes, but what *is* it?"

"I'm going to collect all the clues relating to the crime on this board and then I'm going to look for links," Odelia explained. "That way I might be able to make connections I wouldn't otherwise make. At least that's the theory. I'm not sure how it works in reality."

"I think it's a brilliant idea," said Harriet. "I've always been a very visual cat. I need to see things before I decide what's what and you're exactly the same, Odelia."

"I am," Odelia agreed.

And she was. It was all fine and dandy mulling things over in your head but there were only so many elements you could juggle before losing the thread. And since there were so many suspects in this case she needed to make things visual to make sense of them all.

She started by writing the name of the victim in bold at the top of the whiteboard. Then, underneath, she neatly wrote the names of all the people involved—starting with the seven suspects who'd been identified as having been present around the time Ackerman died. She decided not to include Gran or Mom or Dad, even though they'd been at the library. There was no way they were involved. Even Uncle Alec agreed on that.

There was movement behind her and when she looked up she saw that Gran had walked in through the sliding glass doors.

"Can't sleep either?" she asked.

Gran shook her head. She was looking even more crusty than usual. "I hate it when I can't sleep. I can just feel my face getting wrinklier and my skin drying out like a mummy's. What are you doing?"

"It's called a vision board," said Brutus. "It's what real detectives like Odelia use."

"Oh, right. Like what cops use. They call it an evidence board, though."

"Achoum!" said Brutus in agreement.

"Oh, dear. Do you have a cold?" asked Gran.

"Achaa!" Dooley sneezed, as if in response.

"We better take them to Vena's," said Gran.

Four cats groaned. Going to Vena's was agony to them.

A rustle at the window announced that one more person had decided to join them.

"Hey, Mom," said Odelia. "Can't sleep either?"

"It's this Ackerman business," said Mom. "I haven't slept a wink since I saw his... body." She gave a quick quiver to demonstrate how she felt about finding bodies of dead writers in her library—or anywhere else for that matter. "I can't help feeling people all think that I did it."

"Nonsense," said Gran firmly. "Nobody thinks that, Marge."

"I walked down to the General Store yesterday and I swear people were actually whispering behind my back. And when I tried to talk to Ida Baumgartner she ignored me."

"That's because Ida Baumgartner has a crush on Tex," said Gran. "Everybody knows that."

It was obvious that Mom didn't, judging by the way she sucked in her breath. She then seemed to notice for the first time that Odelia was scrawling strange scribblings on a whiteboard. She moved closer. "Why are those names written in red?"

Odelia tapped the whiteboard. "Darius Kassman, Aldo Wrenn and Sasha Drood. These are our most likely suspects. Wouldn't you agree, Gran?"

Gran had plunked her bony frame down on a chair and was inspecting Dooley, much to the latter's exasperation, as Gran dug her fingers into his tummy and underneath his chin. "Mh?" she said, looking up. "Oh, yeah, right. Most likely suspects. Sure thing, hon."

"Darius Kassman stalked Chris Ackerman and approached him in spite of the restraining order. He struck me as mentally unstable and could have killed Ackerman in a fit of rage. Then there's Aldo Wrenn, or Aldo Ackerman as he now calls himself. Claims he's Chris's son and if he's right he just might share in the writer's substantial inheritance. And finally Sasha Drood, the man who robbed Chris and might have killed him in a struggle."

"Tough," said Gran. "So many suspects. How to determine who did it?"

"And what about Chris Ackerman's wife and son?" asked Marge.

"Chris was still alive after they left," Odelia explained. "They claim Malcolm Buckerfield saw them leave."

"Rockwell Burke said the same thing," Gran pointed out. "Which seems doubtful."

"Not necessarily," said Odelia. "If Malcolm Buckerfield arrived just as Rockwell Burke changed his mind about going in, he could have met him and then met Angelique and Trey as he walked into the library." She wrote, 'TALK TO BUCK-ERFIELD' and added five exclamation marks, then five more for good measure.

"Has *anyone* talked to this publisher?" asked Mom.

"Not yet. He drove home after delivering his final plea to Ackerman."

"And home is…"

"Boston. He's agreed to fly in today, though, and talk to Uncle Alec. So then we'll know more about what he was doing there and why he didn't stick around for the reading."

"I would have liked to meet him. He's almost as famous as the writers he publishes."

"So basically we have three likely suspects and four iffy ones," said Gran.

"And don't forget about the pizza guy," said Max.

Odelia pointed at him. "Thanks, Max. I'm going to track him down today."

"Imagine the pizza guy did it," chuckled Gran. "Because Ackerman wouldn't tip him."

Odelia scribbled 'pizza guy' in the margin. She was nothing if not thorough. She stepped back to admire her handiwork. "So what does this teach us?" she asked her audience.

"That we're screwed," grunted Gran. "All these people could have done it for various reasons and we have no way of figuring out who did do it." She threw up her hands. "Jessica Fletcher makes it look so easy on TV! Only takes her fifty minutes to find the killer—ninety minutes in the movies."

"Aurora Teagarden, too," muttered Max.

"Follow the pizza boxes," Dooley added, quite incomprehensibly.

They all stared at the whiteboard for a moment. Finally Harriet said it best when she announced, "We still have a long way to go, people. *Achee!*"

CHAPTER 33

The visit to Vena's would have to wait. The call came at eight o'clock, just when they were all sitting down for breakfast. Tex, who'd finally noticed the house was empty, had drifted over, and was sucking down his first cup of coffee of the day, slowly waking up. Odelia had baked pancakes, Mom was demonstrating her omelet skills, and Gran showed the others what a superb waffle batter should look like, when Uncle Alec called.

Turned out Chris Ackerman's publisher had flown in the night before and had rented a large beachfront mansion and had invited Uncle Alec to interview him there. Alec had told Chase and Chase had suggested they bring Odelia along, seeing as she was also working the case, albeit in an unofficial capacity. And since Gran wouldn't hear of sitting this one out, she decided to come, too, as well as the fearsome feline foursome, who weren't going to let a little cold stand in their way. Finally, as the library was still closed, Mom was also game.

The only one who wasn't coming was Tex, since he had

patients to attend to. And neither did he mind. Unlike the women in his family, he wasn't bitten by the sleuthing bug.

And so it was that Odelia's pickup was pretty packed as it tootled along the road, Odelia in the driver's seat, Gran riding shotgun, with Marge and the cats in the backseat.

"Nice," said Gran. "Like a family trip to the beach."

"This is still a murder investigation, Gran," said Odelia.

"So I can't enjoy this? You've got to lighten up, dear."

Odelia directed a quick look through the rearview mirror. The thing was that she worried about her mother. People were talking, and they would keep on talking as long as the person who killed Ackerman hadn't been identified, arrested, and tried for murder. Some people would probably keep on talking even afterwards, but that was just because they liked talking and didn't have anything better to do. Luckily they were a minority. The sooner this investigation was over, though, the sooner Mom would be off the hook.

Max, Dooley, Harriet and Brutus were sniffling quietly.

"I scheduled an appointment, you guys," said Odelia. "We're going over there as soon as this interview is over, okay?"

"Okay," said Max thickly.

"Oh, poor babies," said Mom, and yanked a few paper napkins from the dispenser and busied herself with wiping their noses and the liquid flowing from their eyes.

"I feel terrible," Dooley intimated. "And here I thought Jesus would save us."

Odelia frowned. "I forgot to ask. What's with this Jesus business?"

"Shanille baptized us," Max explained. "She figured it would heal Brutus's red spots."

"They're bigger than ever," Brutus grumbled. "Wanna see?" Without waiting for confirmation he jutted out his chest and Mom took a closer look.

"Oh, my," said Mom. "Those are some nasty spots, Brutus."

"Yeah, very nasty," muttered Brutus with gruff satisfaction.

"So… Shanille baptized you?" asked Odelia.

"Yup. In St. John's Church's baptismal font," said Max.

"She dunked us," said Harriet. "Can you believe that? I'm still wet."

Odelia shook her head. She probably should keep a closer eye on her cats. She usually trusted their judgment but this baptism business definitely was not a good idea.

"Maybe we should remove those cat flaps," Gran suggested, who was clearly thinking the same thing.

"Noooo!" cried the four cats in unison, and Odelia laughed.

"Relax. We're not going to remove the cat flaps. But you have to promise us to take better care of yourselves. Use your heads."

"It seemed like a good idea at the time," Max muttered, then sneezed again.

They'd finally arrived at the house where the publisher of Chris Ackerman's books was holed up. It was one of those typical Hamptons mansions, with a high wrought-iron gate, guarded by two beefy security people, a long and winding drive through immaculately manicured grounds and ending in a circular courtyard where the house stood. A three-story structure in pink brick with plenty of gables and windows, the place had a fairytale look.

"Is this where Walt Disney used to live?" asked Dooley admiringly from the backseat.

"The Disney princesses, more like," said Harriet, equally impressed.

Several caterer's vans were parked in the driveway, and white-aproned personnel was hauling stuff into the house.

"Looks like someone is having a party," said Mom.

"Maybe that's for us," said Gran. "I shouldn't have eaten that last pancake. I should have known these rich folks would treat their guests like royalty."

"Pretty sure this isn't for us, Gran," said Odelia as she got out.

Behind them, another pickup rolled to a stop. Chase was behind the wheel, Uncle Alec next to him.

"Looks like the gang is all here," said Chase as he ambled up. He bent over and planted a quick kiss on Odelia's lips, which she happily returned. Since their interrupted dinner date the other night they hadn't had two minutes together. She hoped that by the time the investigation was wrapped up, the film festival would still be in full swing and she and Chase could finally check out that Cary Grant movie.

"So how are we doing this?" asked Uncle Alec, who seemed to have second thoughts about driving up here en masse. "We can't all go in there and crowd the poor shmuck."

"Whatever he is, he's definitely not poor," Gran commented as an ice sculpture was carried out of a moving van by four bulky dudes.

"I suggest Chase and Odelia interview the guy," said Uncle Alec. "While I look around and talk to some of the staff. In my experience staff often know more about what's going on than the principals themselves." He cut off Gran, who'd opened her mouth to protest, with, "You talk to the kitchen staff while I talk to the household staff. Marge, you… mingle."

Mom arched her eyebrows. "Mingle?"

Uncle Alec gestured at a procession of cars that was roaring up the drive. They were all in the high-class category. In other words, the category Odelia couldn't afford. "Looks like the party is about to get started. Talk to the guests and see what you can find out about the relationship between Ackerman and his publisher."

"Aye aye, sir," said Mom with a two-fingered salute.

Uncle Alec displayed a lopsided grin. "We'll meet back here in an hour."

"Shouldn't we synchronize our watches?" asked Gran.

"Only if you're James Bond and you're about to save the world," Alec deadpanned.

CHAPTER 34

"Mingle," said Harriet, then sneezed violently. "How can we mingle when we're standing with one foot in the grave?" She sneezed again, then once more for good measure.

"We'll be fine," I said. "It's just a cold. We'll be right as rain in no time."

"Please, Max," said Brutus with a pained expression. "No mention of water."

At my mention of the word 'rain' Dooley had subjected the skies to a critical look. When no dark clouds heralded in the coming apocalypse, he seemed to relax.

"I can't believe we tried to prevent Brutus from having to visit Vena and now we end up all going to Vena's," said Harriet, checking her precious white fur for spots.

"I'm sorry, you guys," said Brutus. "This is all my fault."

"Personally I blame Shanille," said Harriet. "And next time I see her I'll give her a piece of my mind she won't forget. Jesus, forsooth."

I laughed, tickled pink that Harriet would use such a

quaint expression. But when she fixed me with a haughty glare, I quickly stopped. "I think we better split up," I said.

"Yes, I think we better," Harriet agreed icily.

I had the distinct sensation she blamed me in equal measure as Shanille. She probably figured I should have stopped Brutus instead of encouraging him. Then again, how was I to know that Jesus would smite us with a viral infectious disease that affects the upper respiratory system—if smite is the word I want? Maybe this was a test. But a test of what?

Harriet and Brutus moved off in one direction while Dooley and I moved in the other.

"Do you think Jesus will save us from the apocalypse now that we're baptized, Max?" asked Dooley.

"No idea, Dooley," I said. Unlike Shanille I'm not an expert on matters of theology. "Though I can't imagine he'd let us die in a fiery furnace, considering we went to the trouble of being dunked headfirst in that icy cold water."

"It was pretty cold, wasn't it? Father Reilly should use warm water. Much nicer."

"I'll tell him when I see him," I said.

"You will? Super," he said, greatly gratified. Like I said, Dooley doesn't do irony.

We watched as Odelia and Chase disappeared into the house, while Uncle Alec, Gran and Marge took the small stone path that led around the house—the same direction some of the caterers had taken.

"Have you noticed how much like Jesus Chase looks?" asked Dooley now.

I hadn't, but now that he mentioned it, he had a point. If Chase decided to grow a beard, he'd be the spitting image of Jesus.

This gave Dooley an idea. "Do you think Chase *is* Jesus?"

"I doubt it, Dooley. I think Chase is just a dude."

"How can you be so sure?"

"I…" Actually, I wasn't. How do you know if a dude is just a dude or not?

"What if he *is* Jesus, Max?" he said excitedly.

"Well, that would be pretty cool," I agreed.

A resolute look stole over Dooley's features. "We're going to have to find out."

"And how are we going to do that?"

He nodded knowingly. "Sheep," he said.

"Sheep?"

"Jesus loves sheep. Haven't you noticed that in all the pictures Jesus is holding a sheep? So if Chase is Jesus I'll bet he's got a sheep stashed away somewhere. So all we need to do is find Chase's sheep and then we'll know."

"I don't know," I said dubiously. Even though Dooley's story seemed to make sense, I had the distinct impression there was a hidden snag. I just couldn't put my finger on it.

"I'm going to find that sheep," said Dooley decidedly.

We moved in the direction Grandma, Marge and Uncle Alec had disappeared. Right now sheep were the last of our worries. We needed to find a pet belonging to Malcolm Buckerfield and we needed to find it pronto. I just hoped it was a cat and not a teacup piglet or Yorkie. Nice enough though they were, it's always easier to converse in one's own lingo.

We'd arrived at the back of the house, and I was duly impressed by the scene that greeted us: long tables had been set up, where administrating caterers dressed in white were placing dishes, cups and plates and the other paraphernalia of a garden party. I saw bowls of punch, trays of amuse-bouches and an outside bar where a snazzy-dressed bartender was practicing his cocktail-making skills. A DJ was spinning tunes at a low volume to the far end of the garden, where a dance floor had been set up. This clearly had all the makings of a great shindig, and the guests who were streaming in seemed to agree.

"Nice," I said.

"A little inappropriate," Dooley said with a disapproving frown.

"Why is that?"

"Malcolm Buckerfield was Chris Ackerman's soon-to-be-ex-publisher, right?"

"Right."

"Chris Ackerman died two days ago and here his publisher is holding a party. Seems indelicate to me, not to say downright unkind."

Dooley had a point. It was indelicate. In fact it was suspicious. The man obviously was so happy that his most famous author had died that he was throwing a party to celebrate the fact. "You know, I hadn't looked at it that way," I said, "but you're absolutely right."

Dooley looked pleasantly surprised. "I am?"

"Yes."

He nodded thoughtfully. "I think it's the baptism. It's made me more intelligent."

I would have responded with a choice remark but at that precise moment I finally saw what we were looking for: a black-and-white striped cat slinking along the garden's perimeter. "Target located, Dooley. Let's move in."

Dooley followed my gaze, then nodded determinedly. "On it, Max."

As one, we moved in the direction of the feline. Judging from the way she locked eyes with me, she'd spotted us. Only when we reached her, she seemed coy, eluding us by quickly shifting back to the house, where once again she awaited further developments.

We changed course and made a beeline for the striped cat,

only to watch her tiptoe off, this time jumping up onto a windowsill then gracefully draping her tail around her butt.

"She's toying with us, Dooley," I said.

"You'd think she doesn't want to talk to us," Dooley observed.

"You take the left, I'll take the right," I said, deciding that a little military strategizing appeared to be required here. We did as planned, but once again the wily creature escaped capture by jumping up onto a nearby drainpipe and quickly scooting upwards.

Dooley and I met at the foot of the drainpipe and stared up at the elusive cat. By then she'd reached the roof and sat staring down at us.

"She's making fools of us, Max," Dooley said.

And she was. As I explained, cats don't smile, but this cat was clearly having fun at our expense. "There's only one thing to do," I said.

"I know," said Dooley. "Let's give up."

"What? No! Let's climb this drainpipe," I countered.

Dooley checked the drainpipe, then glanced up, then down again at me. "No way, Max. We're sick cats. We can't be expected to perform a series of complicated acrobatics."

"It's not complicated. We simply climb this drainpipe and we'll have her cornered."

"I don't think this is a good idea, Max."

I decided to play my trump card. "What would Jesus do, Dooley?"

This made him think a bit. "I'm not sure. Maybe we should ask Chase."

"Jesus would climb this pipe. I just know he would."

Dooley didn't look convinced.

"Fine," I said. "Then *I'll* climb this pipe."

And I did, fully expecting Dooley to follow my lead. Only

when I'd reached the second floor and looked down, I saw that Dooley was still on the ground, staring up at me.

"I'm sorry, Max!" he cried. "I thought about it and I figure Jesus would stay put and look after his sheep."

"Dooley!"

"Everybody knows sheep can't climb, Max!"

Oh, for God's sakes... I quickly scooted up that pipe, wanting to get this over with. And I'd finally reached the roof when I saw that the cat was patiently waiting near the chimney, this time giving no indication she was about to escape capture again.

"Hey, there," I said suavely. "My name is Max."

She threw me a sly look over her shoulder, then looked away again.

"Um... nice view, huh?" I said, glancing at the landscape surrounding us. It was pretty stunning. I could see more cars zooming up the driveway, rolling hills of green all around, and not a cloud in the sky. If I wasn't mistaken I would have said the mansion was located right next to a golf course, which would make sense. For some reason rich people like to kick a little white ball and then chase it. Just like dogs. They also love chasing balls. Silly business.

"Who are you?" finally asked the female. She had one of those sultry voices.

"Like I said, my name is Max and—"

"I got that. What are you doing here?"

"Oh, I'm a feline sleuth," I said. "My friends and I are trying to figure out who killed—"

But she was quick to stop me by placing a paw on my face and effectively interrupting my flow of words. "Let's not waste time by flapping our gums," she said in a sexily hoarse voice. "Our eyes met in the crowd. You followed me. I think we both feel it."

"Feel... what, exactly?"

"Oh, Max," she cooed. "You know."

"Know what?"

"Oh, Max," she repeated, then proceeded to give me a head bump.

"Um…"

To my surprise, she suddenly turned and started smelling my butt!

What happened next is one of those things you tell your grandkids about on those long winter evenings when there's nothing on TV. It all went so fast it was over before I knew it. She pressed her nose against my butt, and in a reflex action I folded down my tail to protect this most sensitive area and effectively shielded it off from her inquisitive sniffing. Call me a prude but I don't usually allow strange females to sniff around down there.

She didn't take it well. A dark look came over her face, she produced a loud hissing sound, and before I knew it she'd given me a kick that send me skipping across the roof.

And then I was going over the edge, plunging headfirst into the abyss…

CHAPTER 35

*O*delia was impressed by the high ceilings, the intricate molding, the crystal chandeliers and the parquet floor. She was even more impressed when finally the man they'd come here to meet graced them with his presence. Malcolm Buckerfield was a large man, both in length and girth. He was also a man who had no qualms about showing off his facial hair. Apart from a russet mustache he also sported a perfectly landscaped white beard, a white buzzcut covering a bullet-shaped head and thick black eyebrows. Taken together, practically the full acreage of his head was covered with some type of fur, leaving only his cheekbones, eyes and brow without the benefit of coverage.

"Detective Kingsley," boomed the man in a deep voice. "Miss Poole. Thanks for coming all the way out here to Avalon."

"Avalon?" asked Chase. "Like King Arthur?"

"Myes," said the publisher. "I like to grace every residence I stay at with the moniker Avalon. Like Air Force One, which is only called Air Force One when the President is aboard."

"Oh," said Chase.

"So what can I do for you?"

They'd taken a seat in the salon, Odelia nervous about her shoes soiling the Persian rug and her bottom creasing the green velvet sofa cover. It was like being granted an audience with the Queen of England at Buckingham Palace. Or King Arthur at Avalon.

"You were Chris Ackerman's publisher for thirty years," said Chase.

"I was, yes," Buckerfield acknowledged. "I was very sorry to hear about his death. He was a great writer and a good friend."

"He recently indicated he was changing publishers," Chase continued.

"He was."

"You weren't happy about that."

"I wasn't. He was my most popular author."

"Is that why you visited him two nights ago at the Hampton Cove library where he was holding a reading of his latest novel?"

Buckerfield's eyes flickered beneath those black brows. "How did you—" He gestured with a beringed hand. "No matter. Yes, I did show up at the library. I wanted to give him one final chance to change his mind."

"You made him a very generous offer," said Odelia. "A ten-book contract."

The publisher nodded. "He said he'd think about it."

"He didn't summarily refuse your offer?"

The publisher shuffled uncomfortably in his seat. "No, he did not. Chris and I have known each other a very long time. I published his first novel. I effectively discovered him and gave him his first chance when no one else would. He was simply playing hardball. Up the ante and get a higher advance for his next series of books. That was all this was."

"Are you sure about that?" asked Chase. "Isn't it true that

Chris was having an affair with Stacey Kulcheski, who now works as an editor for Franklin Cooper? And isn't that the main reason he was changing publishers? On the instigation of his new girlfriend?"

Buckerfield bridled. "Nonsense. Chris would never allow his personal life to interfere with his business affairs. Like I said, this was simply a negotiation technique."

"And it worked," said Odelia.

"Ostensibly it did," the publisher agreed. "I never believed for one minute he was leaving us. We have an entire team devoted to Chris. He had no reason to look elsewhere."

"So you didn't get into a fight with him and kill him?" asked Chase, cocking an eyebrow.

"Certainly not! How ridiculous. Chris and I were old friends. I would never hurt him."

His statement didn't strike Odelia as duplicitous. In fact he seemed shocked at the accusation he killed his friend. She decided to try a different tack. "Angelique and Trey Ackerman claim they saw you at the library. They were leaving as you arrived. Is this true?"

Buckerfield nodded. "Yes, it is. I was surprised to see them, to be honest. Chris had made no secret that he'd started divorce proceedings."

"So he was serious about his affair with Miss Kulcheski," said Chase.

"He was. Deadly serious. Pardon me," he quickly added, realizing the insensitivity of his choice of words. "Chris and Angelique's marriage was in trouble long before Chris met Stacey. So it didn't come as a great surprise when he told me what was going on. Angelique didn't take it well, and neither did Trey, who'd chosen to side with his mother and resented his father a great deal. It pained Chris but there was nothing he could do about it. The heart wants what it wants." He gave them a sad smile. "And to think I introduced Chris and

Stacey at BookExpo America last year. BookExpo America is the largest book fair in the States. I could see Chris and Stacey hit it off immediately. Never in my wildest dreams could I have foreseen it would lead to this." He touched the silk scarf around his neck and tugged it thoughtfully. "You'll probably think it's very insensitive of me to organize this party."

"The thought had occurred to us," Chase said with a nod of the head.

"I planned this months ago. Impossible to call it off. Only now I'll dedicate the gathering to Chris. I've prepared a commemorative speech. A eulogy if you will." He unearthed a folded up piece of paper from his vest pocket and fumbled with it for a moment before returning it. "I'm going to miss Chris. He really was a good friend."

"One more question," said Chase. "Do you remember seeing Rockwell Burke? He says he left as you arrived."

Buckerfield grimaced. "I do. I told him not to leave. He'd promised to moderate the event and I thought it cowardly of him not to go through with it. He seemed to have made up his mind, though. Said he didn't want to be accused of selling out by making nice with Chris Ackerman, who he seemed to consider his mortal enemy."

"And when you arrived Chris Ackerman was still alive," said Odelia musingly.

"And so he was when I left," Buckerfield insisted. He glanced at his watch. "And now if you'll excuse me. I really have to attend to my guests. If you want to stay, please do." He waited for a moment, and when Chase nodded his assent, he gratefully rose to his feet and walked out with surprising alacrity and grace for a man of his substantial bulk.

"So what do you think?" asked Chase.

"I think he's telling the truth," said Odelia.

"I think so, too. Which means…"

"Angelique and Trey Ackerman are off the hook, and so is Rockwell Burke."

"Now if only we could determine who of the other three is the man we're looking for…"

And they were both lost in thought for a moment when suddenly loud screams came to Odelia's ear. They seemed to come from outside, and when she got up to look through the salon window, she saw that Buckerfield's guests all stood staring up at something.

"What's going on?" Chase asked as he joined her.

"No idea."

Chase opened the window and leaned out, looking up. "Oh, hell," he said.

A jolt of premonition sliced through Odelia. "What is it?"

He retracted his head. "It's Max. He's dangling from the gutter."

CHAPTER 36

*I*know, I know. Cats don't usually dangle from gutters. And I wasn't! I was dangling from a protuberance. Some thingamajig jutting out of the wall. Possibly an ancient piece of flagpole or lightning rod or what was left of a bust dedicated to the manor's original owners. At any rate, the iron rod—whatever it was—had effectively saved my life. The striped cat's kick had taken me by surprise to the extent that I'd gone over the edge without having the presence of mind to stick out a paw when I whizzed past the gutter and into the precipice.

By the time my survival instincts finally kicked in, I was one floor down, with the ground rising up fast. In desperation I'd grabbed at the wall, and that's when this rod turned up out of the blue and I managed to save myself. The bad news was that I was now dangling between the second and third floor, with no way to go but down. Cats may be capable of gravity-defying feats of acrobatics but we're not exactly Spider-Man. We can't scale walls!

So there I was, wondering how I was going to save myself

from my predicament when suddenly a window below me opened and Chase's head appeared.

"Hey, buddy," he said.

"Hey, Chase," I said, even though I knew he couldn't understand feline.

"Now how in the hell did you get up there?"

I could have told him but instead I produced the kind of plaintive mewling sound people have come to expect from cats in great trouble. Firemen used to saving cats from trees know the kind of mewling I'm talking about, and clearly Chase got the message.

"Listen, just jump, okay?" he said. "I'll catch you."

I gave him a doubtful look. Yeah, right, that look indicated. What if at the last moment he retracted his arms and said, 'Just kidding!'

Not that I didn't trust Chase but he's human, after all, and humans are notoriously unreliable. One minute they stuff their faces with cake and chocolate and the next they're on the treadmill, swearing never to touch sugar ever again in their lives, before starting the whole cycle once more two days into their diet.

"Um…" I said.

"Jump," Chase said encouragingly, holding out his arms. "I got you."

"I don't know about this."

"Trust me."

"Trust him, Max!" Dooley bellowed from below.

I looked past Chase and saw Dooley staring up at me. And so were Harriet and Brutus and a big crowd of people, practically all of whom were pointing their smartphones at me, filming the whole thing. Oh, great. This was going to go viral, wasn't it? There went my reputation. I'd be the talk of the town for months to come, and not in a good way.

"Jump!" Dooley repeated. "He's Jesus!"

And that did it. For one thing, how long was I going to be able to hold on? Not very long. And then what? The fire department would show up with their ladders and I'd have to be saved by a fireman. I'd been through the process before and even though I loved firemen word would spread and even before the fire truck arrived all of Hampton Cove would come running, with their smartphones and then I'd be the laughingstock of the nation.

"He's Jesus!" Dooley repeated, and that did it.

I closed my eyes and I jumped.

Moments later I landed safely in Chase's arms.

He looked down at me, his features backlit by the sun. Like a halo of light.

"Jesus," I muttered. "It's really you."

"See?" Chase asked with a smile. "I told you I'd catch you."

"Max!" Odelia cried. She was inside, right next to Chase, and took me over.

"He's Jesus," I said, still under the influence of the vision I'd just had. Chase stood in the window, that halo of light now illuminating his long hair and his perfectly shaped face.

"I'm so glad you're all right," said Odelia, burying my face in her hair.

But I only had eyes for Chase. "Why did you shave your beard, Jesus?" I asked. "No wonder I didn't recognize you. You shaved your beard to walk among us undetected."

Chase patted my head. "You're all right, little buddy," he said. "You're all right."

"I am now," I agreed. "I am now."

And then Chase took me over from Odelia, walked over to the window and held me up for the crowd below to see. They all broke into loud cheers and applause.

I gotta tell you, it was a real Lion King moment, only better. I mean, come on. Jesus!

Once we were downstairs again, we were greeted like

rock stars, people flocking around. Man, oh, man. It was a real eye-opener for me. So this was what it felt like to enjoy your five minutes of fame. I kinda liked it. A real ego-boost, let me tell you.

Finally, things settled down, a band began to play, and the party kicked into higher gear, with Odelia, Gran, Marge, Chase and Uncle Alec standing together, discussing clues and suspects and whatnot. Harriet, Brutus and Dooley also gathered around.

"So what happened, Max?" asked Brutus.

"I was kicked off the roof by a femme fatale and saved by Jesus," I explained, giving them the CliffsNotes version of events.

"That's great," said Brutus, a little doubtfully. "So what did you find out?"

"That Odelia is one lucky lady," I said. "What did you find out?"

"Nothing much," said Harriet. "Apart from the fact that I don't like caviar."

"They have caviar?" asked Dooley.

"Sure. They've got everything."

"They sure do," said Odelia quietly, her face suddenly heaving into view. She then proceeded to distribute sizable morsels of the most delicious fish dish I'd ever tasted. "There's more where that came from," she promised. She then tapped my nose. "How are you feeling, flyboy?"

"Great," I said. "Thanks to Chase."

"He's something else, isn't he?" she said, smiling.

"He's the best," I said, also smiling.

"Does he have a sheep?" asked Dooley.

But Odelia had already moved out of earshot, on a mission to procure us more food. People were dancing, the band was rocking, and I was starting to experience that mellow feeling that comes upon you when adrenaline levels start settling down. I could suddenly feel a nap coming on, and so when our humans started drifting towards the cars, I didn't complain. The entire drive back I slept like a log, and so did Dooley, Harriet and Brutus. I'd always wondered what divine intervention looked like, and now I knew it firsthand. Though I'd call it Chase Intervention instead—after my hero and savior.

Odelia was one lucky woman. And I was one very lucky cat. And I was still basking in that warm and fuzzy glow when the car suddenly jounced to a halt and Odelia announced in chipper tones, "Wake up, you guys. We're here!"

When I glanced out the window I recognized where we were and promptly broke out in a cold sweat.

Oh, no.

Vena's!

CHAPTER 37

"So what have we here?!" boomed Vena.

I cringed, and so did the rest of the cat contingent. Vena has that effect on cats. She has a big voice, an even bigger personality, and resembles The Rock in more ways than one. She stood before us, hands planted on her hips, a mass of muscle and hearty good cheer.

"They've got a cold," Odelia intimated.

"Yeah, they've been sneezing and coughing all day," Gran chimed in.

"The poor dears," Marge added.

"Let's have a look," said Vena. Without effort, she picked me up and plunked me down on the operating table. I fully expected her to start probing me with all manner of metal implements before plunging some type of syringe into my neck but instead her surprisingly gentle touch and warm hands performed a quick but thorough examination.

"Mh," she said. "He's got a cold, all right, but only a minor one. Nothing to worry about." She gave me a tickle behind the ears. "You'll be right as rain in no time, Max."

"Oh, that's great news," said Odelia.

"Thanks… Vena," I said, surprised to get off so easy.

"You're welcome, buddy," she said, almost as if she could understand what I said.

"See?" said Gran. "I told you not to worry."

"I didn't worry," I said indignantly.

"No, but I did," said Dooley.

"Dooley is the worrier of this little gang of cats," said Odelia with a smile.

In short order, my friends underwent the same treatment, until finally Brutus was on the table.

"He's got spots," said Odelia. "So you may want to look at those."

"Spots?" asked Vena. "What spots?"

"Red spots. On my chest," said Brutus. "Do you think it's cancer? Am I going to die? I was baptized last night. Shanille said Jesus would save me but I'm not sure she wasn't full of crap. She's the reason we got this cold, you know. She dunked us into this gigantic vat of ice water and now I feel worse than ever, so—"

"Stop babbling, Brutus," said Harriet.

Brutus abruptly stopped babbling.

"He has spots on his chest," said Odelia, translating Brutus's gibberings. "Red spots."

"Probably been drinking," said Gran. "What?" she added when Marge rolled her eyes. "Pets can have a drinking problem, too. You should have seen my husband's dog Rex. The two of them always went on their benders together. Came home drunk as skunks."

"I don't have a drinking problem," Brutus said indignantly. "Teetotaler all the way."

"It's so funny the way your cats talk, Odelia," said Vena with a smile.

"Yeah, they're real talkative," said Gran. "Blabbermouths, the lot of them."

"I wonder where they get it from," Marge murmured.

"Let's check those nasty spots, shall we?" Vena said, and parted Brutus's fur like Moses the Red Sea.

Brutus giggled. "You're tickling me," he laughed.

"Mh," said Vena finally. "Myes. I see what you mean. Spots. Red ones."

Brutus stopped giggling. Instead, a look of panic came over his face. "Oh, no!" he cried. "It's cancer! She's going to put me down! Please don't let her put me down! Save me! I'm too young to die! Don't let me dieeeeee!"

Odelia smiled indulgently but didn't respond. Long experience has taught her it's unwise to be seen talking feline in front of other people. Even veterinarians. Especially veterinarians. They might put her down instead. "So what do you think?" she asked.

"Pollen!" Vena boomed.

"Pollen?"

"Pollen! Nothing to worry about."

"But I thought pollen affected the eyes and nose?"

"Not with cats it doesn't. Pollen leads to atopic dermatitis, also known as skin allergy." She gave Brutus a pat on the head. "Which is what this fellow is suffering from. Usually the rash will appear on the outside of the ears, on the head, face or paws. In this big fella's case it manifested on the chest. Nothing that some medication won't take care of."

"That's great," said Odelia, clearly greatly relieved.

"Wait, I'm not going to die?" asked Brutus.

"No, you're not," I said. "Just an allergy. To pollen."

"What's pollen?" asked Dooley.

"It's the yellow powdery stuff you find inside flowers," I said.

"Huh," said Brutus. He looked down at Harriet. "Babe! I'm not going to die!"

"Of course you're not going to die," said Harriet, looking

peeved. "Making a big fuss about nothing." And she stalked off, her tail high. But when she passed me, she gave me a wink. She might not have shown it, but I knew she'd been worried about her mate, too.

And while Vena discussed Brutus's treatment with Odelia, I happened to glance up at a shelf that was littered with Thank You cards from grateful pet owners, boxes of medicine samples, plush cats and dogs and all manner of pet toys. It also contained a mock-up of a hamburger—the popular dog toy. It was one of those plastic hamburgers, looking pretty realistic, too, and instantly reminded me of Big Mac. And as I stared at the hamburger, I was suddenly struck with an idea so novel and riveting that I momentarily forgot where I was. Only when Odelia told me it was time to go did I become aware of my surroundings again.

All the way home I found myself lost in thought, and by the time we arrived at Casa Odelia I'd made up my mind about the course of action to take. I could have told Odelia but I thought it was probably better to check out a few things first. And I knew exactly who to ask.

CHAPTER 38

*T*hat night, a soothing blanket of darkness and silence had draped itself across the happy little town of Hampton Cove, that jewel in the Hamptons crown. Revelers were enjoying the nightlife in places like Southampton, East Hampton or Montauk, but here locals slept the sleep of the peaceful. So did Odelia who, after a long and strenuous day, enjoyed the warmth of her comfy bed and would have enjoyed it even more if not a strange voice had suddenly started competing with the sweet dreams she was entertaining.

She frowned, the blanket of sleep rudely ripped apart, and opened her eyes.

"I found a love," the voice was whining. *"Darling just dive right in."*

She instantly recognized it as Ed Sheeran's *Perfect*, only this obviously wasn't Ed Sheeran straining his vocal cords but some amateur caroler. Or it might have been a cat undergoing a thoroughly painful castration.

She winced as the unknown singer transitioned into the

second verse, effectively massacring poor Ed's beautiful ode to love.

Neighbors left and right had also caught on, and voices now competed with the singer, shouting such encouragements as, 'Shut up!' and 'We're trying to sleep here!'

Finally, Odelia couldn't suppress her curiosity any longer, so she got out of bed and padded over to the window. She peeked through the curtains and when her eyes landed on the lanky male figure standing under her window, singing his heart out, she gasped in shock.

The Ed Sheeran wannabe was none other than… Chase!

She threw the curtains wide and opened the window.

When Chase saw her appear, he smiled and redoubled his efforts to butcher the song. And then the first boot landed. It landed at Chase's feet and he stared down at it for a moment, not comprehending. The second boot hit him against the shin but only when a third projectile hit him in the face did he finally get the message.

"You better come in," Odelia said quickly, not wanting her boyfriend to be pummeled with a waffle iron or Crockpot next.

Chase looked a little dazed but staunchly refused to back down. Going into the song's final stretch, he belted out those last few notes with a zeal and a fervor possibly better reserved for a nobler cause. Still, it touched Odelia's heart that he would do such a thing for her—expose himself to bodily harm to serenade her like an old-world troubadour.

The final note died away, Chase smiling up at her.

And then he was hit with a skillet and went down hard.

"Oh, crap!" Odelia cried and hurried down the stairs. Racing out into the backyard, she knelt down next to her knight in shining armor—which he could have used at this point—and saw that he was shaken but conscious.

"Odelia," he said, a smile curling up his lips. *"You look perfect tonight."*

"Oh, Chase," she said. "Thank you so much. That was... lovely."

It was, after all, the thought that counted, not the execution.

From next door, Marge and Tex's faces had appeared in their bedroom window.

"Way to go, Chase!" Tex yelled, giving the singing cop two thumbs up.

"Wonderful song choice, Chase," Marge said, wrapping her nightgown around herself.

"Thanks, Marge," he said. "And I've got your husband to thank for it."

"Who threw the skillet?" asked Gran, her head stealing out from her bedroom, like a turtle out of its shell. She'd probably waited until the sky stopped raining kitchen paraphernalia.

"Never mind the critics. You did great, son!" Tex cried.

"Give the kids some privacy, Tex," said Marge.

Three heads retracted back into their homely shell and then it was just Odelia and Chase and the big canopy of stars in that great expanse of sky overhead.

"Do you want to come inside?" she asked.

"I thought you'd never ask," said Chase with a grin.

As he got up, he rubbed the spot on his noggin where the skillet had impacted.

Once inside, Odelia sat the wannabe Ed Sheeran down on a kitchen stool and inspected his head. "You'll have a nice bump," she said after a cursory check.

"It's worth it," he growled and dragged her onto his lap, then planted a kiss on her lips. When she came up for air, she was feeling dizzy. He might be a lousy singer but he was a great kisser.

"So my dad put you up to this, did he?" she asked.

He became serious. "There's something I wanted to talk to you about ever since your grandmother moved out. I just wasn't sure how to launch into it. And since our dinner date was interrupted by this Chris Ackerman business..." He shrugged. "I just figured your dad might have a few tips for me."

"Tips for what?" she asked.

"Odelia Poole," he began, his gold-flecked eyes turning molten. "I'm not a man who minces words so here goes." He'd clasped her hands in his and she discovered she was holding her breath. "There's not a doubt in my mind that you're the one for me—the woman I love. And I've been thinking it's time for us to take the next step. To take this to another level. So what do you say we officially move in together? Technically I'd be the one moving in with you, as the alternative would mean you moving in with me and your uncle."

She smiled. This was a no-brainer. "Yes, I would love to move in together, Chase."

He grinned and then they kissed and little angels popped out all around and blew their little trumpets and sang their little hearts out. And not a single skillet zoomed through the air.

Finally, they let go and Odelia looked around. Something was missing from this scene and she suddenly realized what it was. Her cats. They were nowhere to be found.

Probably wandering about in the park. She couldn't wait to tell them. Judging from the way Max and Dooley had taken a shine to the burly cop, they'd be over the moon.

She took Chase's hand in hers and gave him a coy look. "Wanna check out your new digs, Detective Kingsley?"

"Don't mind if I do, Miss Poole," said Chase.

And as they headed up the stairs, she imagined the look

on Max and Dooley's faces when they finally arrived home and found Chase in Odelia's bed. She smiled at the thought.

CHAPTER 39

ot for the first time I decided to engage cat choir in my sleuthing efforts. So Dooley and I—along with Brutus and Harriet—headed down to the park to enlist our friends in the scheme I'd worked out while driving home from Vena's. As I'd expected, they were all game, and so the search began. I just hoped that not too much time had passed since the fateful events at the library. By now two whole days had passed, and Hampton Cove's council had strict rules about garbage collection so our window of opportunity just might have closed.

Dooley and I had decided to search in the immediate vicinity of the library, while the other cat choir members looked along ever-widening circles. If my hunch was right, before this night was through we should be able to come up with something.

Brutus, who seemed reborn after Vena's diagnosis, was our most enthusiastic searcher, along with Harriet, who, in spite of her initial grumblings, was happy as a clam.

"So you think Brutus will be all right?" asked Dooley as he tentatively checked the dumpster closest to the library.

"I think Brutus will be just fine," I returned. "Especially with Vena's treatment."

"You know? I'm starting to think that Vena may not be our enemy, Max."

I'd been thinking the same thing. Our visit had been distinctly painless and even—to some extent—enjoyable.

"Maybe she's not out to hurt us," Dooley continued.

"Only the future will tell," I said, jumping down from the dumpster. I didn't enjoy this consequence of my crazy theory. And if I was wrong a lot of cats were going to hate my guts.

Dooley had caught on, too. "What if we don't find anything, Max?"

"Then we'll probably get kicked out of cat choir." Again.

"I don't mind. You're my friend and I will always stand by you," said Dooley.

The unexpected statement gave me pause. "Aw, Dooley. You're my friend, too."

"You know—when the apocalypse finally comes, I hope we won't be ripped apart by the tsunami's massive waves and terrifying mayhem. Or by the hot lava that will push up through the earth's cracked crust. When finally the end comes, I hope we'll die in a blaze of fire and destruction together. Wouldn't that be just great?"

Great wasn't exactly the word I'd use to describe Dooley's predictions. I decided to try one more time to change his mind. "Look, the apocalypse may never happen, Dooley."

"Oh, I know," he said to my surprise. "But you don't really believe that, do you?"

"Actually, I do. I think everything is going to be just fine, buddy."

Dooley smiled. "Oh, Max, I love you but you're so naive. You believe everything you see on the internet. All these disinformation campaigns. All that fake news. It would be funny if it wasn't so sad. No, you have to start checking out some of this *real* news. Like the fact that a comet is on its way to earth right now and will hit us in exactly three days."

I shook my head. Absolutely hopeless. Just like our search in Hampton Cove's dumpsters. Maybe this wasn't such a good idea after all. And now Shanille would be upset that she'd skipped a cat choir rehearsal to prove my crazy theory.

Just then, a familiar cat trotted up to us. It was Clarice.

"Dumpster-diving, Max?" she asked.

"Um, not exactly," I said.

She directed an icy look at me. "You do know that this is my territory, right?"

"I... thought this was Big Mac's domain?"

"Not exactly. I *allow* Big Mac to scavenge here. First he asked me for permission, though—and agreed to pay me my usual fee. Fifty percent."

"Fifty percent..."

"Of his haul."

"We're not looking for food," said Dooley. "We're looking for clues!"

Clarice narrowed her eyes. "Clues."

"We could give you fifty percent of our clues," Dooley suggested, "but first we have to give our clues to the police. They're going to need them to put the bad guys away, see?"

Clarice didn't appear particularly interested in fifty percent of our clues, though. She made a dismissive sound. "You can keep your clues, city slicker."

"You could help us," I said as she started to walk away.

She threw me a skeptical look over her shoulder. "Me? Help *you*?"

"There's fresh pizza in it for you," said Dooley. "Barbecue chicken pizza."

Her upper lip rose in a snarl. "Do I look like the kind of cat who eats junk food?"

To be honest she looked like a cat who gobbled down rats and other vermin whole.

"We can get you anything you like," I said, sweetening the deal. "Anything at all."

"I already have everything I like." She gestured around. "All the food I need. Fresh air. My freedom. So what could you possibly offer that I'd be even remotely interested in?"

"How about your own bowl, your own cat bed, your own nook in our house?"

Clarice eyed me suspiciously. "Your human already offered me free passage into your home. To come and go as I please. Unlimited access to her food supply."

"Yes, but now you would get your very own space in your very own home."

It was a grand offer, but I wasn't at all sure she would go for it. Then again, Clarice was an unpredictable cat, so there was no way to know how she would react.

Finally, that inscrutable expression seemed to thaw. "Home," she muttered.

"Uh-huh."

"My own bowl."

"Yup. And your own bed."

The silence stretched on for a moment while she pondered this. She gave me a skeptical look. "You're not pulling my paw, are you, cat? Because you know what I can do with even one paw tied behind my back. Or three."

"Oh, no! I would never pull your paw."

"Fine," she growled. "I'll take it."

"Great!" I cried, much relieved.

"Not that it matters much," Dooley decided to put in his two cents. "Since the world is ending in a couple of days you won't have much time to enjoy your new home anyway."

Clarice decided to ignore this outburst. "Follow me," she snarled.

We followed her. She took us around the corner to a row of large round trash cans with lids. She walked up to the third can in the row and reached up to give the lid a shove. It clattered to the ground. Then she stood to the side and casually started to lick her paw.

"Look inside," she said.

I looked inside. And there it was. The holy grail. The clue I'd been looking for.

CHAPTER 40

*O*delia woke up and wondered why it was still dark out. She blinked confusedly and looked around with a heavy heart. Realizing it wasn't her heart that was heavy but that something was pushing down on her chest, she realized it was Max sitting on top of her.

"Odelia!" he was saying, trying to keep his voice down. "Wake up! We found it!"

"Found what?" she muttered, still sleep drunk.

"The proof we need to take down Chris Ackerman's killer!"

At these words, she was suddenly wide awake. "What?"

"We found it!" he repeated. "In a trash can!"

"In a trash can," Dooley echoed from the floor next to the bed.

Odelia sniffed. There was something rancid about the air in her room.

"Do you smell that?" she asked.

"Oh, that's us," said Harriet, seated next to Dooley.

"We've been dumpster diving," explained Brutus, also part of the small troupe.

"It was Max's idea," said Dooley.

"But I showed them where to find the thing," said a fifth cat.

Odelia stared at this newcomer. She was small, she was scruffy-looking, and she looked vaguely familiar in the moonlight streaming in through the window.

"You remember Clarice," said Max. "I said she could stay here if she wanted to."

"Only as a last resort," said Clarice. "And only in case I run out of fresh rats."

Odelia wrinkled her nose. "Um… Guys? Could you tell me what's going on exactly?"

Next to her, Chase stirred, then murmured, "What's going on with your cats, babe?"

There was a momentary silence, then Max asked, "What is Chase doing in your bed?"

"Yes, what is Jesus doing in your bed?" asked Dooley.

"We decided to move in together," she said.

"Are you talking to your cats?" asked Chase. "Cause it sounds to me like you are."

"Go back to sleep, honey," she said soothingly. "I'll go and give them some… milk."

"You do that. And tell them to shut up and let us sleep," Chase mumbled.

Odelia threw off the duvet and swung her feet to the floor. "Follow me," she whispered, then tiptoed out of the room, the small clowder of cats following in her wake. Once downstairs, she flicked on the light in the kitchen and plunked herself down on the couch, yawning freely. "Now tell me all about it."

And Max and the others did. "First off, I promised Clarice a cat bed and her very own bowl," he said.

"Done," said Odelia.

"She's the one who found the thing," he explained.

"Great work, Clarice."

"Thanks," Clarice said grudgingly. She directed a suspicious look at Odelia. "But don't think for a minute that this means I'm domesticated. I'm a wild cat and that's the way I'll stay."

"Fair enough," said Odelia, conceding this point. "What else?"

"My spots are practically gone," said Brutus happily.

"Nobody cares about your spots, Brutus," Harriet snapped.

"Great news, Brutus," said Odelia, wondering if this was the reason they'd dragged her out of bed. "Cat bed for Clarice and spots are clearing up. Super duper. That's it?"

"Tell her about the thing!" Dooley said.

"I am telling her!" said Max. "Though I probably better show you," he added.

"Show me? Show me what?"

Max hesitated. "Are you up for a little drive?"

§

When finally Odelia found herself looking down the trash can Max had singled out for her attention, she had to admit he'd outdone himself this time.

"Amazing," she said. "Are you sure about this?"

"Pretty much," said Max. "It was the fake hamburger, you see."

She didn't, but she nodded anyway. Then she took out her phone. "I better wake up my uncle. He's going to want to check this out."

"What about Chase?" asked Max.

"There's no way I can tell Chase that my cats found the

key piece of evidence in Chris Ackerman's murder investigation," she said.

"So what are you going to tell him?"

She smiled. "I'll think of something. Uncle Alec! Sorry to wake you. You're not going to believe this…"

&

*A*s it was, Uncle Alec did believe it. Long association with Odelia and her cats had taught him that nothing was impossible when it came to their powers of observation and keen deduction. He arrived five minutes later, looking as if he'd just rolled out of bed, which probably he had, his shirt untucked and the few remaining hairs on his head standing up.

"Where is it?" he asked, and when Odelia gestured to the trash can, he took out an evidence baggie and stared down at the piece of evidence Max had unearthed—or Clarice. The story was still a little fuzzy to Odelia.

"I think you're going to need a bigger bag," she said.

"I think you're right," he said. "Your cats found this?"

"My cats found this."

"Huh. I guess I won't be putting *that* in my report."

"Not if you don't want to freak out my new live-in boyfriend you won't."

Alec grinned. "I knew he'd pull it off."

"He told you about the Ed Sheeran thing?"

"Are you kidding? He practiced on me first. The kid's got crazy singing skills."

Odelia decided not to dissuade her uncle from this conviction.

Chase had a lot of skills, but singing wasn't one of them.

"So what happens now?" she asked.

"Now we send this off to the lab and see what comes back."

"You better check all the CCTV cameras in the area."

"Oh, I'm going to—don't you worry about that."

He took out a bigger baggie, a pair of tweezers, and plucked out the item, then deposited it into the baggie with a look of satisfaction on his face. "Nailed it," he grunted.

"Not yet. We still have to identify—"

"Trust me, I will. You go on home. You've done enough."

"But—"

"Go home, Odelia. Give your boyfriend a wake-up kiss. I'll handle the rest."

And he stalked off, an officious swagger to his hips, got into his car and drove off.

"That's it?" asked Max.

"That's it," said Odelia.

"But... who did it?"

"I think I have a pretty good idea. And I'm going to prove it."

Of course she could have let her uncle take care of things, as he'd indicated, but where was the fun in that? Besides, this was her investigation, and she was going to see it through to the end—whatever her uncle said.

CHAPTER 41

*C*hase woke up in an empty bed, his hand touching the spot where Odelia had been when he went to sleep. The spot was cold. He rubbed his eyes and groaned. He vaguely remembered some middle-of-the-night cat emergency, and Odelia slipping out of bed to feed them milk. So had she stayed up and gone straight to work? Or was she downstairs, still officiating the cat's convention? To be completely honest, he wasn't all that big on cats. Not that he was a cat hater, per se, but he'd never understood the extreme lengths cat lovers would go to to appease their furballs.

When he felt movement near his feet, he glanced down and saw that those furballs were fast asleep at the foot of the bed: four cats lying in a row. He had to admit, when they were sleeping like this they looked peaceful enough. Cute, even.

"So where's your master, huh, cats?" he asked.

Max opened his eyes and he could have sworn the big red cat not only understood the question he'd posed him but was actually answering in lazy tones! Huh. Weird.

He got out of bed and sauntered to the staircase. "Odelia?" he yelled from the top of the stairs. "Are you down there?"

When Max suddenly appeared next to him and meowed some more, he started.

"What are you trying to tell me, buddy?" he said, then laughed at his own silliness. Cats were dumb creatures. Mousers, by and large, with some minor capacity for entertainment. He picked Max up and carried him down the stairs. "Are you hungry?" he asked, setting him down in the kitchen. A row of bowls sat on the floor, five in a row, and all of them featured names and were filled to capacity. So Max was definitely not hungry.

The little guy kept meowing up a storm, though, and since Chase had no way of determining what the heck he was trying to tell him, he merely grinned and decided to take a shower and start his day. Arriving upstairs, he saw that Chief Alec had left him a voice message. As he listened, his eyebrows rose. "What the…" he muttered.

There had been a breakthrough in the case, and he'd slept right through it!

"Christ," he said.

This seemed to attract Dooley's attention, who looked at him almost reverently.

"Hey, buddy," he said. "Max is downstairs, Odelia is nowhere to be found, and I gotta run. Think you'll be able to take care of yourself?" Then he laughed. "You big dummy! Now you're talking to cats!"

He walked into the bathroom. Time for a quick shower and then he was off. He actually felt pretty excited about moving in. Time to put this relationship with Odelia on a more permanent footing. Soon he was enjoying the cascade of water and loudly singing the only song he'd ever memorized in his life. Ed Sheeran's *Perfect.*

I was truly worried about Odelia. She'd given us the slip and now she was out there somewhere, chasing the bad guys with no backup from her legion of felines. I just hoped she would be careful. Odelia has a tendency to go all gung-ho without considering the consequences. When she's on the hunt she sometimes forgets that the people she's hunting are dangerous killers and creeps and would just as happily turn on her if it suited them.

And I'd just settled down in front of my bowl and gulped down a few tasty morsels when a loud panting sound reached my ears. Fully expecting Brutus, I didn't even look up. But when the panting sound was replaced with stertorous breathing, I said, "Try to breathe through the nose, Brutus, not the mouth." I hate mouth-breathing cats, don't you?

"Huh?" said Brutus, only when I didn't recognize his gruff voice I finally looked up and discovered it wasn't Brutus but Big Mac breathing down my neck!

"Big Mac! What are you doing here?"

Probably all the pizza we'd fed him had led to him coming back for more.

"It's your human!" said Big Mac. "I think she might be in big trouble."

"What are you talking about?"

"I was downtown just now, staking out the Hampton Cove Star hotel, when suddenly I saw your human head inside. So I went in after her, and followed her all the way upstairs. She went into a room and never came out. Also, when I put my ear against the door, I heard people arguing and I heard your human yelling. And then she went quiet. Too quiet!"

A cold grip squeezed my heart. "What do you mean she went quiet?"

"Just that. First she was yelling and then she stopped. I think she might be dead."

"Better lead the way, Big Mac," I said, then hurried to the foot of the stairs and bellowed, "Dooley, Brutus, Harriet! Come quick! Odelia is in trouble!"

Cats have this amazing capacity to be awake and alert in an instant. No snooze button for us. When the game is afoot, our ears prick up and we're ready to go at the drop of a hat. And so it was now. Seconds after I'd issued my cry for help, three cats came racing down the stairs. And even as Chase was murdering poor Ed Sheeran in the shower, we were shooting through that cat flap, Big Mac in the lead, the four of us right on his tail.

"How did you get to be at the Hampton Cove Star?" I asked as we hurried along through the backyard.

"Pigs," he said, panting.

"Pigs?"

"Okay, I admit it! I love the McRib even more than the Big Mac! And since the McRib contains pork, I wanted to see those piglets you mentioned to see what my food looks like before I eat it!"

Yuck. Who wants to eat a piglet? "They're teacup piglets, Big Mac," I said. "They're not fit for feline consumption."

"You eat piglets?" asked Harriet censoriously. "You're an animal, Big Mac."

"I am!" he cried. "I admit it. I *am* an animal."

We'd arrived at the house next door and I scooted in through the cat flap, then up the stairs and into Gran's room.

"Gran!" I tooted into her ear. "Wake up!"

"Don't hurt me, Captain Hook, I'm just an innocent virgin!" she yelled as she shot up and speared open her eyes.

When she saw it was me and not Captain Hook, she grunted, "Max—what's the big idea scaring me half to death?!"

"Odelia is in trouble over at the Hampton Cove Star!" I said urgently. "We have to save her!"

"Say no more," she said, removing the hairnet she always sleeps in. She got out of bed and, still dressed in her flannel pajamas, followed me out of the room. Then she seemed to think better of it, returned to her room, and moments later came stalking out again, this time dressed in a pink nightgown tied around her bony frame with a golden sash. Her pale sticks for legs were bare, and she'd shoved her feet into her favorite lime-green Crocs. "Ready to rumble!" she exclaimed, and then we were off.

CHAPTER 42

*O*delia had figured she'd have a nice civilized chat with the person she most suspected of murdering Chris Ackerman. She had a hunch, and as every good reporter knows, not to mention any halfway decent amateur sleuth, you need to follow up a good hunch with some spade-work before you get where you want to be.

So she'd decided to ignore her uncle's creed and head down to the Hampton Cove Star that morning, bright and early, and personally ferret out the truth. When her uncle had messaged her, even as she breezed into the hotel, that blood had been found on the item they'd retrieved, she felt stiffened in her resolve to finally get to the bottom of this thing.

'Check DNA,' she texted back.

'Already on it,' Uncle Alec returned promptly. 'Will keep you in the loop.'

He'd better keep her in the loop. She was the one who'd landed this piece of evidence in his lap. Or actually Max had landed it in her lap before she'd clued in her uncle.

Speaking of Max, she suddenly became aware of a large

cat trailing her into the hotel. And when she looked down, she saw that it was none other than Big Mac, the cat who'd provided them with the initial breakthrough in the investigation. He glanced up at her, then gave her a fat wink. She smiled, wondering what he was doing here all by himself.

"Are you by any chance visiting the pigs?" asked Big Mac.

"Um… yes, as a matter of fact I think I am," she said.

"Can I join you? I've never seen a pig before. At least not a live one. I've seen pigs as the finished product—also known as the McRib—but they tell me it's not the same thing."

"Sure. Just follow me."

As they rode the elevator up in silence, she wondered what Chase would say about her habit of chatting with cats. He'd probably think she was crazy.

"The meat is really succulent," Big Mac was saying. "Pork, I mean. I'm sorry if I'm babbling. It's just—I like food. A lot. I guess I'm one of those whatchamacallits—a connoisseur?"

"That's fine," she said. "We all love food."

"Yeah, but I *love* love food," he stressed. "Like, food is my main passion."

She smiled. Big Mac was a little weird but he was also adorable. "You look a lot like Max," she said.

"Yeah? I'll take that as a compliment."

"You should."

As the elevator halted to a stop, the thought briefly occurred to Odelia that maybe—just maybe—she should have told Chase what she was up to, but then her phone chimed again and when she read the new series of messages, she smiled knowingly. *Yesss!*

She knocked on the door and patiently waited. When Angelique appeared, she smiled a pleasant smile and said, "I'm sorry to disturb you at this early hour, Mrs. Ackerman, but I wonder if I might ask you a few more questions. This time it's for my article."

"Oh, sure," said Angelique. "Come on in."

The excitement of the hunt had her fully in its grip now, so when she closed the door behind her she totally forgot about Big Mac, leaving him languishing in the corridor.

"Miss Poole!" said Trey Ackerman. "To what do we owe the pleasure?"

Only now did Odelia notice the paper-thin scar slicing the young man's brow. It gave him a sinister aspect. "Just collecting some more background information for my piece."

"Oh, that's right, you're a reporter as well as a police consultant. Please take a seat."

She did, seating herself in an overstuffed chair near the window, while Angelique took the second chair across from the small antique table and Trey remained standing.

Suddenly Odelia felt a little uncomfortable and crowded, but she bit back the sentiment. "We talked to your ex-husband's publisher," she began, "and he confirmed that he saw you leave as he arrived."

"That's great news," said Angelique, glancing up at her son. "That means we're finally off your radar, right?"

"Well…" She swallowed, then decided to take a different tack. "Malcolm Buckerfield also confirmed that he offered Mr. Ackerman a new contract, and that Chris was seriously considering his offer. So it looks like Mr. Buckerfield is off the hook as well."

"But as I understand it you have other suspects, right?" said Trey. His mother had reached out a hand and he pressed it. "This, um, robber, and then there's the crazy stalker and of course you have met the fellow who insists he's my father's son."

"Which is nonsense, of course," said Angelique. "If my husband had an affair with this woman he would have told me."

"Yes," said Odelia. "I suppose he would have. Only, it's all about motive, isn't it? That's what it all comes down to, over and over again."

"Motive and opportunity," Trey agreed, nodding. "So these three men, they had both. And now the police has the unenviable task of figuring out which one of them is the real culprit."

"I very much doubt whether Sasha Drood had sufficient motive," said Odelia. "He's a thief, not a murderer, and even though he's been in jail plenty of times, he wouldn't want to go to jail for murder. Not a man like him. Then there's Aldo Wrenn, who claims Mr. Ackerman was his father. But why would he kill him? All he had to do was prove his claim and he would be set for life."

"You're forgetting that if he really is my father's son he stands to inherit a part of the inheritance," Trey pointed out.

"My uncle talked to Chris Ackerman's attorney this morning, and according to the stipulations in his will your ex-husband left the bulk of his fortune to Stacey Kulcheski."

This was clearly news to Angelique and her son. "What?!" cried the woman.

Odelia nodded. "I'm afraid so. And Aldo Wrenn knew about this. Chris's lawyers told him as much. Aldo wouldn't get a penny, even if he was his son. So Aldo knew he'd never benefit from his father's death. Only in the event that Chris stayed alive could he hope to effect a reconciliation, get into his father's good graces and possibly earn himself a place in his will. So there goes his motive as well."

"He could have flown off the handle and committed murder out of spite," said Trey.

"He's not the type," Odelia said.

"So what about this stalker? He's obviously crazy and extremely dangerous."

"We've just received confirmation that Darius Kassman is actually Stacey Kulcheski's cousin. He developed an obsession with your ex-husband after being introduced to him by Stacey at her home. Darius may have been obsessed, but he isn't dangerous. Stacey vouches for him. Said he would never hurt a fly, and most definitely not her future husband."

"Nonsense," Angelique exclaimed sharply. "Of course she would say that. You want to know what I think? Stacey put him up to this. This Darius Kassman is a vulnerable young man and she manipulated him into murdering my ex-husband. Especially considering the information you just gave us concerning his will."

She clearly wasn't happy about this turn of events. Odelia leaned in. It was now or never. "Mrs. Ackerman—can I speak to you in private?"

Trey got the message. "I'll be in the next room," he said, swiftly removing himself.

"What is it you wanted to talk to me about?" asked Angelique, a little stiffly.

"It's about your son," said Odelia. "We found a discarded pizza delivery outfit in a trash can near the library. We found blood on the shirt that we think matches your ex-husband's blood type. A DNA test will be carried out, both on the blood and the shirt, which I believe will put Trey at the scene of the murder. Which means... he killed his father."

"What are you talking about? What preposterous nonsense!"

"I'm only telling you for your own protection, Mrs. Ackerman. Trey killed his father and I'm afraid your life may be in danger as well. Which is the real reason I came here."

Angelique stared at her for a long moment, then suddenly burst into laughter.

"Oh, you're such a naive little wench, aren't you, Miss Poole? Trey—come back here!"

"No!" Odelia said, jumping up from the chair. But Angelique pushed her back down.

"You're not going anywhere!" the woman snapped, and suddenly Odelia discovered that she was holding a small silver revolver in her hand, with the barrel pointed at her heart.

"Silly, silly girl," said Trey, who'd come up behind her and now placed his hands on her shoulders. "Did you really think I'd go to all this trouble without talking to my dear, sweet mother first?"

"Trey adores his mother, don't you, Trey?" asked Angelique, still pointing that revolver at Odelia. "So when he saw that I was suffering such terrible abuse at the hands of his father, he suggested we do something about it. And so the plan was hatched, and carried out to perfection."

"Thank you, mother," said Trey appreciatively.

"You should have burned that outfit, though."

"Beginner's mistake?" said Trey, a smile sneaking up his pale face.

"It doesn't matter. We'll be out of here and on our way to Mexico before these silly little small-town cops put it all together," said Angelique. She directed a mocking look at Odelia. "Of course I knew Chris didn't leave me a single penny. He told me. Which is exactly the reason we emptied out his bank accounts last week, transferring all of his money into an account Trey set up in the Cayman Islands. I had to pay Chris's accountant a hefty sum but it was definitely worth it. Chris was the one who didn't have a penny, not me. If he was going to leave me for that stupid editor of his I was going to make him pay. Big time."

"Let me guess. You left Chris that night, making sure you were seen," said Odelia, "only for Trey to return later, dressed as a pizza guy. Where did you get the outfit?"

"Stole it from some local pizza parlor that same night," said Trey. "Easy peasy."

"Weren't you afraid to get caught?"

"Nah. Nobody pays attention to the pizza guy. I could just as well have been invisible. I saw that Drood creep on my way out, but I quickly ducked into an empty room and waited him out." He chuckled—a terrifying sound. "I figured he'd make a perfect scapegoat and he did."

"Too bad about the outfit," said his mother.

"Can't be helped, Mom. If I'd burned it, someone would have seen."

"You could have brought it back here. We could have disposed of it together."

"What's done is done. Next time we plan a murder we'll pay more attention to the details." A slow smile crept up his pale face. "So how do *you* want to die, Miss Poole?"

CHAPTER 43

*O*delia sat trussed up in the small bedroom. Two piglets were staring at her. Unfortunately for her she could speak feline but she couldn't speak pig. Not that it mattered, for her mouth was taped up with heavy-duty electrical tape and her hands and feet were tied up as well. She'd read somewhere that pigs have very sharp teeth, so they could have set to work freeing her of her restraints. Instead, they just sat there on the bed staring.

She sincerely hoped that Trey Ackerman had been kidding when he told her that parting gag about murdering her. She did not feel like dying, especially now that her life was slowly coming together. Chase was moving in, her cats were all in good health, and she still had both her parents and her crazy grandmother.

Speaking of Gran, she suddenly thought she heard her voice.

Then the door was thrust open and Gran came walking in! More accurately put, Gran came flying in, landed on the floor and then the door was closed behind her.

"Hey, you brute!" Gran cried, balling her fists. Then she

spotted her granddaughter. "Odelia! There you are! I thought they'd already filleted you like a fish."

She crawled to an upright position and crossed the room.

"Are those pigs?" she asked.

"Get me out of this tape!" Odelia cried. Though it sounded more like, "Wepmeouoheeape!" It's tough to enunciate clearly when your lips are taped up.

"Hold your horses," said Gran. "I'm getting there. This tape is pretty sticky."

It took the old woman a while, but finally she managed to yank the tape off.

"Owowoowwww!" Odelia cried.

"Oh, don't be a baby. Just think of it as a lip waxing. Saves you the trouble to do it yourself. Now how the hell did you get mixed up with those murdering bozos?"

"I could ask you the same thing!" said Odelia, removing the tape from her around her feet.

"I came here to save you, little missy. I didn't think they'd have a frickin' gun."

"You should have called Uncle Alec. Or Chase. Now we're both going to die."

"I don't think so. When I arrived they were packing up. I think they're moving out."

"Trey asked me how I wanted to die!"

"He was probably kidding. He looks like a kidder."

"Gran, he dressed up like a pizza guy then killed his own father in cold blood."

"Yeah, well, that wasn't nice," Gran admitted.

"We've got to get out of here. Let's check the windows."

They checked the windows. The room they were in was located on the second floor facing the back wall of another building. Too high to jump, and no one in sight they could shout for help at.

"Terrible view," said Gran. "If I were the Ackermans I'd

have lodged a complaint. Who wants to look at that horrible wall all the time?"

"I'm sure they don't mind!"

"And I'm sure they do. Even killers mind about stuff like that, honey."

"New plan. I'll hide behind the door, and when they come in to kill us I'll rush them!"

"They won't come in. They'll pack up and get out of here and by the time housekeeping finds us they'll be long gone and on their way to Mexico."

Odelia had to admit her grandmother was probably right. Why add two more murders to their resume when they could simply flee and live out their lives spending Chris Ackerman's millions?

She sank down on the bed, causing the two piglets to bob up and down.

"They *are* pigs," said Gran, taking a seat next to her. "How about that?"

&.

"Hurry up, will you?!" Angelique shouted. "If they catch us they'll put us in jail and throw away the key."

"Relax, Mom. They won't catch us." Trey gestured with his head to the connecting door. "What about those two?"

"Leave them."

"We could shut them up forever."

"When did you suddenly turn into a character from a Quentin Tarantino movie?"

"I guess it's true what they say about murder. You develop a taste for it."

"Yeah, well, better develop a taste for escape. I want to go now!"

Suddenly he pricked up his ears. "Do you hear that?"

There was a sound outside unlike anything he'd ever heard. It tickled his funny bone. It sounded like Ed Sheeran but not. More like someone was murdering the ginger singer.

"I love that song," he said. "But whoever is singing it clearly hates it."

He moved over to the window and looked out. Down below, some musclebound moron was belting out the notes like nobody's business. He didn't seem to care that traffic had ground to a halt and that people were leaning out of their windows to gawk at him. Hecklers were shouting abuse at the guy and children pelted him with rocks but he just kept on singing, oblivious.

"Probably thinks Carson Daly is staying at the hotel," chuckled Trey.

'You suck!' someone shouted, and Trey thought those were his sentiments exactly. This dude, whoever he was, would never get a four-chair turn. Not even a one-chair turn.

"Let's go!" his mother bellowed again.

"All right, all right, all right!" he said, tearing himself away from the scene down below. "What about Kevin Bacon and Miss Piggy? We can't leave without them."

"You should have thought of that before you locked Miss Amateur Sleuth and her granny in there. Now are we leaving or what?"

He hated to leave his pigs. He loved the little cuties. And as he moved to the door to the other room, suddenly the door to this one exploded and before he knew what hit him a bunch of cops stormed in and the atmosphere erupted into a free-for-all of shouts and screams and pounding boots and angry faces hollering at him to 'GET DOWN *NOW!*'

So he did. And briefly wondered who was going to take care of his piglets.

CHAPTER 44

*O*delia was still a little dazed as she was escorted out of the hotel and onto the sidewalk. Cop cars blocked traffic and she watched in confusion as the hand-cuffed Angelique and Trey were escorted into a squad car and driven off at a high rate of speed, sirens blaring.

"How—what—when—" she stuttered.

"Oh, didn't I tell you?" said Gran. "Before I left the house I instructed Marge to wake up Chase and send in the cavalry. I figured he might do what he could to save his sweetheart."

Chase came hurrying up to them, and she jumped into his arms, happy to be alive.

"For a moment there I thought I lost you," Chase intimated.

"For a moment there I thought so, too," said Odelia.

"Oh, don't be a bunch of saps," said Gran, which was rich for a woman who loved her soap operas more than anything else. "We're all fine and the bad guys will be punished so all is well that ends well. Now what's going to happen to those little guys?"

She was pointing to a cop who was holding two piglets in

his arms. He had a mustache and his name tag indicated that his name was Jackson. Odelia recognized him as the cop who wouldn't let her into the library the night of Chris Ackerman's murder. He didn't look happy to have been awarded the particular task of taking care of Trey's piglets. Especially since his colleagues were busy snapping selfies with him. He was going to become the latest Hampton Cove PD social media sensation, that much was obvious.

"Don't worry about the pigs," said Chase. "We'll find someone to adopt them."

Uncle Alec walked up, looking distinctly unhappy. "Odelia Poole," he said gruffly. "What part of 'I'll handle things' don't you understand? You could have gotten yourself killed, young lady, and your grandmother in the process."

"I just figured Angelique was innocent and wanted to warn her."

"Next time do as you're told," he said sternly. "When Marge called me with the news that you were in trouble I almost had a heart attack." He wagged a stubby finger in her face. "Never again, all right? Have mercy on your uncle's poor ticker."

"I won't do it again," she promised, seeing now how foolish her actions had been.

"Oh, don't get your panties in a twist, Alec," said Gran. "I was there. We were fine."

"They had a gun!"

"I'm pretty sure they weren't going to use it."

"You don't know that, Ma. They could have shot you both."

"Well, they didn't, so now are you going to stop crying in your milk and congratulate Odelia instead? She cracked this case."

Marge and Tex also joined them on the sidewalk, while rubberneckers all around stood taking in the scene. "Honey,

I'm so glad you're all right," said Marge, enveloping Odelia in a hug. "When your grandmother told me to wake up Chase, I feared the worst."

"I wasn't asleep," said Chase, a little indignant. "In fact I'd been up for hours."

"He's right," said Marge. "He was in the shower when I arrived. Gave me a shock."

Chase grimaced at the recollection and Odelia suppressed a grin. She would have loved to have seen the look on Chase's face when Mom walked in on him in the shower.

"The important thing is that the bad guys will get what's coming to them," said Gran.

"How did you find out?" asked Chase. "I mean—how did you know where to find that pizza guy's outfit?"

A momentary silence descended over the small company. Chase was the only one who didn't know about the cats. "Just one of those hunches, I guess," said Odelia. "I suddenly wondered about the pizza guy. See, the weird thing about the pizza boxes that we found at the library was that they were clean. Pizza boxes usually have leftover pizza or ketchup smears or chunks of cheese stuck to them. These boxes were brand new. Never used. So that got me thinking. What if the pizza guy wasn't a pizza guy? What if he was the killer and he'd only dressed up as a pizza guy to throw us off the scent?"

"And then we took things from there," said Uncle Alec. "In all fairness, though, Odelia found the outfit."

"And a good thing I did. Today is collection day in that part of town. A couple of hours later and the outfit would have been gone forever."

"And along with it the blood stains and DNA that will show beyond a reasonable doubt that Trey Ackerman killed his father," Uncle Alec finished the story.

"Hard to believe that a son would kill his father," said Chase, shaking his head.

"I don't think he devised the plan," said Odelia. "Angelique did. Trey just went along with it and did the actual deed—wanting to spare his mother the more gruesome aspects of the scheme she'd hatched. In fact she probably decided to kill her husband months ago, when she discovered he was planning to leave her for Stacey Kulcheski."

"There's only one part about this whole sordid business I regret," said Gran.

"What's that?" asked Marge.

Gran threw up her arms. "That I didn't get to film the grand finale! Those bastards took away my phone!"

"I'm sure plenty of people caught the whole thing on video," said Uncle Alec. He clapped Chase on the shoulder. "For one thing, they sure as heck caught our rising musical star Chase on tape. Ed Sheeran, watch out!"

"Thanks," said Chase. "I kinda enjoyed being the decoy."

"It sure delayed the Ackermans until our team was in place to break down the door."

"Too bad I didn't catch the big performance," said Odelia.

"You saw the private performance," said Chase, smiling. "Which was the better one of the two."

Only now did Odelia realize she was missing something. She looked around. "Where are my cats?"

"Right there," said Chase, stepping aside.

And there they were indeed: Max, Dooley, Brutus, Harriet and… Big Mac. Sitting on the sidewalk and smiling up at her. They were a sight for sore eyes.

"Oh, my babies," she said, crouching down. They all jumped into her arms. "You caught the bad guys—you saved my life—what would I do without you?"

Chase laughed. "It's the weirdest thing. Almost as if they can understand what she says."

"Don't be ridiculous," Gran snapped. "Cats don't talk. Everybody knows that."

"No, of course not," he said, his smile vanishing. "You're right."

"Dumbass," Gran grunted.

"Ma," said Uncle Alec warningly.

"Just welcoming the kid into the family," said Gran, and pinched Chase's cheeks.

EPILOGUE

"So what did you tell Chase when you went to warn him?" asked Odelia.

"Simple. I told him I had a feeling you were in trouble," said Marge.

"But how did you explain I was at the hotel?"

Marge took a deep breath, darted a quick look at Chase, who was assisting Tex with the barbecue as usual, then explained quietly, "I told him I'd once seen a documentary about whales being able to feel their babies were in trouble even though they were miles away. I said the same thing applied to mothers and their kids. I said I could sense you were in trouble and I had a hunch you'd had a hunch about the writer's son and ex-wife."

"Seems far-fetched," said Odelia, taking a bite from her hot dog. "He believed you?"

"Oh, he did. Immediately. You've got a good man there, Odelia. He's a keeper."

They moved off and Dooley glanced up at the sky. It had been a week since the stunning events at the Hampton Cove

Star and the world hadn't ended, which clearly puzzled Dooley.

"Trust me, Dooley," I said now. "The world isn't going to end. I mean, at some point it probably will, but not this week. Not even this year or even this decade."

"You think so, Max?"

"I know so. So you can stop worrying."

"And stop nagging us," Harriet muttered.

"So how about those spots of yours?" I asked Brutus.

"You're not going to believe this but they're gone!" said the black cat. And to prove he wasn't lying, he pressed his chest into my face.

"Nice," I muttered.

The four of us were seated on the swing on Marge and Tex's back porch. Tex was officiating the barbecue, aided and abetted by Chase, Uncle Alec was recounting the story of how Angelique and Trey Ackerman had been charged with murder, and Gran was messing around with her phone, checking the footage she'd shot in the course of the investigation.

"You know? You really outdid yourself this time, Max," said Brutus.

"How is that?"

"I still don't get how you had that sudden brainwave that led you to figure out what happened."

"I told you. It was the plastic hamburger. I suddenly remembered Big Mac going on and on about how the pizza guy wasn't a real pizza guy because he didn't smell like one. So that plastic burger got me thinking. What if Big Mac was right? What if the pizza guy *wasn't* a pizza guy? What if it was the killer *pretending* to be a pizza guy? Which meant he would have ditched the outfit as soon as he got the chance. So if only we could find it—"

"We'd find the killer," Brutus said. "Pretty clever, buddy."

"Max followed the pizza boxes," said Dooley. "Just like Aurora Teagarden."

We all laughed. Dooley was right. The pizza boxes had led us to the killers.

"The real hero is, of course, Big Mac," I said. "He's solved the whole thing."

We all looked in the direction of the big red cat, who was gobbling down the hamburger patties Tex kept feeding him. Finally, he waddled over in our direction. He was too big to jump up onto the swing, so he stayed where he was, then heaved a soft burp.

"And? How do you like the taste of a real burger?" I asked.

Big Mac shook his head sadly. "It's not the same, you guys."

"But these are real burgers—not the junk food you usually eat."

"Yeah, but junk food tastes so much better," said Big Mac. "Honestly? There's no comparison. No offense," he added for Tex's sake.

"He can't understand you," said Harriet. "Only Odelia, Marge and Vesta can."

"Weird. What about the buff dude?"

"Nope. Chase doesn't understand us either."

"Or the sheriff?"

Harriet shook her head. "Only the women in this family speak feline."

"Huh. Too bad. Would be so easy if the whole world could understand us."

"No, it wouldn't," said Clarice, who'd joined us. She'd been coming and going these last couple of days, trying to get accustomed to having her own home. I had a feeling it wouldn't last, though. Once a feral cat, always a feral cat. Odelia had tried to domesticate her once before and it hadn't worked. Then again, Clarice probably wouldn't be the same if she became like the rest of us. That was part of her appeal. And the reason I liked her.

"What are you guys talking about?" she asked now.

"Humans," said Big Mac.

"Oh, don't get me started on humans," she growled, darting a cold look at the humans gathered in the backyard. At that moment Odelia offered Clarice a piece of raw burger. She swallowed it down whole. Odelia laughed and fed her another piece.

"These humans aren't so bad," said Big Mac.

"I guess not," said Clarice grudgingly.

Clarice and Big Mac stalked off, to gobble up some more burger, and Brutus and Harriet followed their example, only to abruptly change course and disappear through the hedge into the next garden. Brutus probably wanted to show Harriet his lack of spots.

"Do you think Clarice will be part of the gang from now on, Max?" asked Dooley.

"Pretty sure she won't. She's a street cat, Dooley. What's more, she rules those streets."

"I don't get it."

"We think Clarice should be saved from her dumpster-diving ways but that's not how she feels about it. She's free out there, the queen of the urban jungle. Sometimes I think it's she who pities us, and not the other way around. Pities our sedentary, domesticated lives."

"I don't get it," Dooley repeated.

"Have you never wanted to roam the streets as a wild cat, Dooley? Not knowing whether you're going to find food or not, but happy with every morsel you do find? Give those old hunting instincts free rein? Become wild and free once more, like our ancestors?"

Dooley stared at me. "Is this a trick question?"

"Haven't you ever wondered if there's another world out

there? A world beyond the safety of our houses, our back-yards, the humans who protect and feed us, even this town?"

He chewed on that for a moment. "Actually, no," he said. "I think we're blessed, Max. Only sometimes we lose sight of the fact. We forget how lucky we are. And it takes events like the ones that transpired last week to bring that truth home to us. It takes Brutus almost dying from his spots and Odelia and Gran almost being shot and the sky almost falling down on us and the earth opening up and swallowing us whole to remember how lucky we are."

I stared at him. "You figured that all out on your own?"

He leveled a funny look at me. "I'm not as dumb as I look, Max."

"I guess you're not," I agreed.

"The thing I've realized this past week is that I'm probably the luckiest cat alive," he said musingly. "I have the best humans, who love me very much—one of them is Jesus, even though I still haven't found his sheep—I have the best buddies, in Harriet and Brutus. But most of all, I have the best friend in the whole wide world. You, Max. I love you, buddy."

"I… love you, too," I said, surprised. My eyes were suddenly moist. I wiped at them.

"Darn cold," Dooley muttered, wiping at his own eyes.

"Yeah, darn cold," I said, sniffling.

We sat in silence for a moment.

Then Dooley held up his fist.

I bumped it.

Boom.

EXCERPT FROM PURRFECT OBSESSION (THE MYSTERIES OF MAX BOOK 10)

Chapter One

I was lying on my back in the backyard, languidly gazing up at the clouds slowly drifting past my field of vision. My paws were dangling wherever they might, my tail was drooping, and it wasn't too much to say that all was well in this best of all worlds.

Some would have called it the calm before the storm, but they would be cynics. This wasn't the calm before the storm. This was the calm after the storm, as there had been rain overnight, and the grass was still soggy and drops clung to Odelia's roses' petals.

Next to me, my best friend and co-feline Dooley lay in the same position, also idly gazing up at the sky. There was apprehension in his gaze, though, his usual response to looking at that big slice of heaven up above. His eternal fear is that a piece of this heaven might one day come crashing down on us. And no matter how many times I've assured him that this is simply impossible, there's no way to dissuade him from these erroneous ideas.

"I don't know, Max," he said now, shaking his head.

"What don't you know?" I murmured, my eyes drifting closed. There's only so much to look at when you're gazing at the sky. It's blue and all looks pretty much the same to me.

"I don't know about this lying around, doing absolutely nothing."

"It's what us cats do best," I said. "We lie around doing nothing."

"But it just feels... wrong, you know."

"No, I don't know. What are you talking about?"

"This ... " He gestured at the sky. "And this..." he added, indicating the smooth lawn that was our favorite hangout spot on a sunny day like this—especially after a nice storm.

"I don't get it, Dooley," I said lazily. "Please elaborate."

"I just don't understand how you can lie around while there's so much to be done."

"Nothing needs to be done," I said, my eyes now having closed completely, my head slumping to the side. I felt a power nap coming on, and nothing Dooley said was going to prevent me from enjoying it tremendously.

"There's probably murder cases to be solved."

"Not a single one."

"Or-or missing humans to be found?"

"Nobody's gone missing as far as I know."

"Dangerous diseases to be fought? Pests to be eradicated? Threats to be thwarted? Max! We can't just lie around here while who knows what is happening all around us!"

"Oh, just relax, Dooley," I muttered, on the verge of tumbling headfirst into sleep.

"Relax! How can I relax when... when…"

But at this point I'd finally found sleep, or maybe sleep had found me? At any rate I'd become blissfully oblivious of Dooley's ramblings. There's only so much angst one can stomach. And it was with extreme reluctance that I pulled myself from the depths of a super slumber when a sharp voice interrupted a sweet dream about a new addition to cat choir, a tabby tease who wasn't merely blessed with great pipes, but was quite the looker to boot.

"Max! Wake up! Something terrible has happened!"

It was Harriet, who's a member of our posse. Immediately, I was up and ready for action. When Dooley is yammering on about all sorts of imaginary threats, I'm not bothered. That's just par for the course. But when Harriet does the same... it means something's up.

"What's wrong?" I didn't even bother rubbing the sleep from my eyes. It's one of the advantages of being a cat: there's never any sleep that needs to be rubbed. One moment we're practically comatose, the next we're shifting into high gear, all at the drop of a hat. Or the flash of a white whisker, as in this case. That's millions of years of evolution for you.

"It's Odelia," said Harriet, a strikingly pretty white Persian. She was slightly panting. With my keen detective's eye, I could tell she'd been running. Or was under duress. Or both.

"Odelia! What's wrong with Odelia?" Dooley practically yelled.

Odelia is our human, and in that sense pretty much our raison d'être one could say. I know, I know. Cats are supposed to be these independent creatures, unattached and unfettered. Don't let our stoic and aloof look fool you, though. We do care about our humans, and we don't like it when something bad happens to them. That's why I was ready to skip sleep and follow Harriet without a moment's hesitation, and so was Dooley.

"What happened to her?" I asked, already fearing the worst.

"Just hurry," said Harriet, and sprinted ahead of us at a high rate of speed. We tore through the backyard, tore through the small strip that separates Odelia's house from her neighbors, and tore out across the front yard. Ours is a corner of the world where people still enjoy living in houses that are detached, semi-detached or even attached. No apartments for us, and a good thing, too. I wouldn't enjoy being an apartment cat.

We were out onto the street and Harriet still showed no signs of slowing down. Already I was breathing heavily. I'm a cat built for cuddles, not for speed. Some people call me portly, but they're wrong, of course. I'm big-boned is what I am. A matter of genetics.

"Where are we going?" I managed between two stertorous intakes of breath.

But Harriet didn't even bother to respond. It just confirmed to me how grave the situation really was. Usually she's the chatterbox of our small clowder of cats, and the fact that she hadn't uttered more than a few words told me this was bad. Very bad indeed.

She tore around the corner and I could tell we were heading for the park, the very place I'd been dreaming about only moments before. Oh, how long ago this now seemed.

"I don't like this, Max," Dooley intimated.

Well, I didn't like it either, but at that point I was too winded to respond. Into the park Harriet zipped, and Dooley and I followed, still going full tilt. We almost bumped into her when she abruptly stopped, and then we just stood there, me panting, she squinting.

"There," she said finally, pointing with her fluffy white tail.

I looked there. And I didn't see a thing.

"What are we looking at?" I asked therefore, scanning the horizon for a sign of a bleeding and grievously harmed Odelia, most probably on the verge of expiration.

"There!" she repeated, this time pointing with her paw.

And that's when I saw it. Dooley must have seen it too, for he drew in a sharp breath.

It was Odelia, only she wasn't bleeding. Worse, she was locking lips with a man.

And this man was not—I repeat this man was NOT… her boyfriend Chase Kingsley.

Chapter Two

"Max?" asked Dooley, his voice croaky and weird. "What's going on?"

"Can't you see what's going on!" Harriet replied in my stead. "That's our human down there, being treacherous!"

Treacherous was not the word I would have used. As far as I know humans are not a monogamous species. Not unlike cats—though some cats have been known to be loyal to their mate until their dying day. Harriet is not one of those cats, so I found her indignation highly hypocritical. I didn't mention this, though, for Harriet's claws are as sharp as her tongue, and I wasn't looking for a lashing of either. Still, I wouldn't have thought it possible for Odelia to cheat on her boyfriend. I'm not an expert on human love, but I'd had the impression true love was involved in this particular pairing of a reporter and a local copper.

"Max! What's going on?!" Dooley practically wailed.

"I think what's going is that Odelia, being human and therefore flawed, is making an error of judgment,'" I said carefully. Dooley is not one of your tough cats. He's sensitive, and situations like these are something he should be shielded from, not encouraged to witness.

I directed a reproachful glance at Harriet, who should have known better than to subject Dooley to this kind of sordid scene. Of course my glance went right over her head.

"She's enjoying it," said Harriet now.

And she was right. Odelia clearly was enjoying this romantic interlude with one who was not her chosen mate.

"I don't like this, Max," said Dooley, not taking this well. "I don't like this at all."

"I don't like it either," I intimated, "but such is life, Dooley. Sometimes the people we think we know best surprise us. And not always in a good way."

Just then, a third person approached Odelia and the unknown male, and spoke a few words. The effect of these was immediate. Odelia extricated herself from her kissing partner and got up from the picnic blanket on which she'd been sitting. She stood, hands on hips, while this third person, another male, seemed to explain something to her. Possibly giving her pointers on her kissing technique.

The scene, apart from the shock effect it had on those who'd become used to seeing Odelia linked in body and soul to Chase Kingsley, was otherwise a peaceful and idyllic one: there was a picnic basket present, a picnic table, and even a dog lying at the lovers' feet.

I did a double take. Wait, what? A dog? Where did this mutt come from? Odelia didn't have a dog. Or did she?

Dooley had spotted the dog, too, for he produced a sound like a kettle boiling.

"Looks like Odelia is moving on," said Harriet, voicing the thought that had occurred to me as well.

"She's getting rid of us and getting... a dog?" I said, now shocked to the core.

"Looks like," Harriet confirmed. "She was petting him before, and he seemed to like it."

I was speechless. Kissing strange men was one thing, but getting a dog to replace her loyal brace of cats? That was too much. No, really! After everything we'd done for her she was getting a dog? This was treason of the highest order. Worse. This was a travesty.

I decided enough was enough, and set paw for the despicable scene.

"Max, no!" Dooley and Harriet cried out, but I paid them no heed. Odelia had gone too far, and I was going to speak my mind and tell her what was what, even at the price of having to be within twenty yards of a canine, which was the limit I usually set myself.

When I approached the picnic scene, Odelia was frowning, listening intently to the second, non-kissing male, a man with a fashionable red beard that curled up at the end, as was the current trend. Meanwhile the kisser was munching on a sandwich, not a care in the world.

The dog was the first one to become aware of my impending arrival, for he lifted first his head, then his upper lip in a vicious snarl.

I hesitated, but decided this mission was too important to be derailed by the pathetic snarls of a cat's mortal enemy.

"Odelia!" I said, deciding to come in strong and pitch my sentiments before she had a chance to become distracted by her lover and the bearded hipster dude.

Odelia looked up, that frown still furrowing her forehead.

"A word, please?" I said, keeping a keen eye on the canine, whose upper lip was trembling now, his eyes shooting menace and all manner of mayhem in my direction.

"Max!" said Odelia, clearly surprised to see me. She quickly shut up. It's not a fact widely known, but Odelia belongs to a long line of women who talk to cats. From generation to generation, this gift is passed, and a good thing, too. For far too long, humans have turned a deaf ear to a cat's desires. Now, with Odelia and her mother and gran to listen to our plea, our voice is no longer ignored. Who also wasn't ignoring my voice was the dog.

"What do you want, cat?" he snarled, his hind legs tensing as he got ready to pounce.

"This doesn't concern you, Lassie," I said, holding up my paw. "So back off."

"This is my terrain, cat," he shot back, tail wagging dangerously. "Get lost or else."

"Or else what?" I asked, sounding a lot braver than I was feeling. Those fangs did not look appealing. Saliva was dripping from them, and already thoughts of rabies and front-page articles about a blorange cat being mauled to death started popping into my mind.

"You don't want to find out," he said with a low growl that seemed to rise up straight from his foul innards.

Odelia, who'd followed the tense interaction, crouched down next to me. "Max," she said quietly, so the kisser and the hipster couldn't overhear. "What are you doing here?"

"I could ask you the same thing," I said, as haughtily as I could. "I saw you," I added. "Canoodling with that... that... man."

Odelia frowned, as if not comprehending what I was saying. Then, suddenly, she laughed! Actually burst out laughing! "Oh, Max," she said, giving my head a patronizing pet. "That's just acting!"

"Whatever it is, it's despicable," I said. Then I frowned. "What do you mean, acting?"

She gestured with her head to the kisser, who now stood chatting with the weird red beard. "That's Don Stryker. He's a New York stage actor. And the man with the beard is Wolf Langdon—he's our director."

And then I remembered. Odelia had mentioned something about performing in something called Bard in the Park, and had even mentioned snagging an important role.

I stared her. "You mean this is all... acting?"

"All of it," she assured me, then took an apple from the picnic basket and took a bite, plunking down next to me. She lowered her voice. "And let me tell you, it's no picnic so far.

This guy's breath… "She rolled her eyes and waved a hand in front of her face. "Hoo-wee."

In spite of myself I laughed. "Garlic. I can smell it a mile away. I thought you liked it."

"No, Max. Women don't like it when men chew a clove of garlic before a big kissing scene. Allegedly that's how Clark Gable annoyed Vivien Leigh in *Gone with the Wind*."

I decided to skip the small talk. I hadn't forgotten about my real beef. "What about that," I said, pointing at the rabid dog, still snarling and softly growling in my direction.

"Scoochie?" she said. "He's in the scene. He's an actor, too."

"The dog is an actor?"

"Sure. Dogs can be actors. Pretty much any animal can be an actor."

This was news to me. Slightly mollified, I asked the most important question of all: "So… He's not going to live with us?"

Odelia laughed again and patted my head. "Silly Max. Of course not. He's going home with his trainer once rehearsals are over. And right now he lives with the rest of the troupe at Whitmore Manor. In his own room. Did you think I'd adopt a dog and not tell you guys?"

"No, of course not," I said, "Don't be silly." But behind her back I gave Harriet and Dooley, who still sat watching from a safe distance, two thumbs up. Or rather, since cats don't have those nifty and very handy opposable thumbs, two claws up at any rate.

"Hey, what's wrong with adopting a dog?" growled the dog.

"Nothing," Odelia was quick to say.

That's how my human is: kind to animals, children and even dogs.

"I thought so," grumbled the mutt.

The man Odelia had identified as the director now turned to her. "I liked what you did there, dahling," he said, "but could you give it a little more—I don't know—oomph?"

"Oh, sure," said Odelia, getting up. "What sort of oomph are we talking about here?"

She began discussing the ins and outs of the oomphs of acting in detail, and I soon lost interest. Instead, I glanced around and saw that a small film crew sat hiding behind a nearby tree. They'd filmed the whole thing! Probably to learn from and correct later.

I just hoped they hadn't filmed Odelia and me chatting. Because that would definitely not be good!

Chapter Three

Odelia watched Max stalk off, his tail in the air, his rear end wagging slightly, and couldn't help but smile. She could only imagine what he must have thought when he saw her kissing Wolf Langdon like that. In the distance, she saw Dooley and Harriet, anxiously awaiting Max's return with news from the front line. Cats were sensitive creatures, who hated change. Kissing a strange man must have spooked them a great deal. Just then, her real-life boyfriend appeared, crossing the plain to where she stood. Don, who'd been snacking on the contents of the picnic basket, saw him coming and a dark cloud seemed to descend over him. "Don't tell me Captain America is going to cause trouble," he said.

"Chase isn't here to cause trouble," Odelia said. She didn't much care for her co-star. Apart from his garlic antics, he was arrogant and not much fun to be around. And he had a habit of sticking his tongue down her throat, even though it wasn't part of the script.

Chase had joined them and gave Odelia a quick peck on the lips. "Hey, babe," he said in that low rumbling voice of his.

He held out a hand to shake Don's, but the actor simply ignored him and walked away, a dirty look on his otherwise handsome face.

"See ya around, Poole," Don muttered, and was off.

Chase retracted the hand. "What was that all about?"

"Oh, nothing. Don has this thing about the boyfriends of his leading ladies."

Chase quirked an eyebrow. "A thing? What thing?"

"He was once on the receiving end of a punch thrown by an actress's spouse. His nose has never been the same."

"He must have given him reason," said Chase, looking on as Don made his way over to the makeup table for a touch-up and a flirtatious chat with the makeup ladies.

"I'd say he did," said Odelia. "Don Stryker has a reputation as a ladies' man, and he likes to make sure that reputation stays earned."

Chase quirked his other eyebrow. "Should I worry about this Stryker guy?"

She smiled. "No, of course not." She draped her arms around his neck and gave him a kiss. "Nothing to worry about at all."

"That's more like it," he rumbled, then lifted her up into a full-body hug. If Don was watching, the hug might be interpreted as a gesture of possessiveness but Odelia didn't care. There was only one man in her life and that was Chase, and no arrogant Broadway star could change that.

"So I was thinking," said Chase now.

"Yes?"

"I was thinking we haven't gone out on a date in a while—just you and me."

She liked where this was going. "So what do you suggest?"

"I suggest dinner and a movie? There's a new place in Happy Bays we haven't tried. It's called The Dusty Tavern and they're rumored to serve some damn fine clam chowder."

"The Dusty Tavern it is, then."

"I have some stuff to finish up at the precinct. Pick you up at the house at seven?"

"Sounds great. See you later, Chase."

"See you, babe," he said with a happy grin, then was off, but not before giving Don the kind of look that would remind him of the punch that had given his nose that tweak.

Odelia sank down on the blanket and took the script she'd tucked underneath the basket and opened it to a well-thumbed page. This was the first time she was playing a part in a play, or any performance, for that matter. She had no acting experience whatsoever, but she didn't mind. It wasn't as if this production would be seen by more than a few people.

Bard in the Park was a strictly local setup, designed to entertain natives and tourists alike. Not exactly the start of a great career in acting. More like a fun way to while away the time and do something different for a change. Also, Dan Goory, her editor at the Hampton Cove Gazette, had instructed her to write a piece on the acting troupe, and the recurrent phenomenon of summer public theater, and what better way to write about Shakespeare in the Park than to immerse herself in its world and even play a small part?

She frowned as she read through her lines. The hardest part about this acting thing was memorizing those big chunks of text. She was constantly in fear she would drop a line and get absolutely, completely stuck, with people all staring at her. Which was why she was determined to study hard and nail her dialogues until she could recite them in her sleep.

And she was still muttering William Shakespeare's memorable and immemorial lines to herself when a loud scream suddenly pierced the air. She looked up, startled, and was even more surprised when she saw a small group of people standing around nearby, the director and some of the other troupe members among them.

She got up and hurried over, afraid someone had become unwell and had collapsed.

When she reached the small throng Wolf Langdon, his face white as a sheet, was already clutching his phone to his ear and barking, "She's dead. She's dead, I'm telling you!"

Finally Odelia reached the commotion. On the ground, her face frozen in a mask of shock, a young woman lay motionless, her eyes staring unseeingly up at the people all crowding around her. It wasn't hard to figure out she was, indeed, dead, what with the big knife sticking out of her chest. Odelia recognized her as Dany Cooper. Her understudy.

ALSO BY NIC SAINT

The Mysteries of Max

Purrfect Murder

Purrfectly Deadly

Purrfect Revenge

Box Set 1 (Books 1-3)

Purrfect Heat

Purrfect Crime

Purrfect Rivalry

Box Set 2 (Books 4-6)

Purrfect Peril

Purrfect Secret

Purrfect Alibi

Box Set 3 (Books 7-9)

Purrfect Obsession

Purrfect Betrayal

Purrfectly Clueless

Box Set 4 (Books 10-12)

Purrfectly Royal

Purrfect Cut

Purrfect Trap

Purrfectly Hidden

Purrfect Kill

Purrfect Santa

Purrfectly Flealess

Nora Steel

Murder Retreat

The Kellys

Murder Motel

Death in Suburbia

Emily Stone

Murder at the Art Class

Washington & Jefferson

First Shot

Alice Whitehouse

Spooky Times

Spooky Trills

Spooky End

Spooky Spells

Ghosts of London

Between a Ghost and a Spooky Place

Public Ghost Number One

Ghost Save the Queen

Box Set 1 (Books 1-3)

A Tale of Two Harrys

Ghost of Girlband Past

Ghostlier Things

Charleneland

Deadly Ride

Final Ride

Neighborhood Witch Committee

Witchy Start

Witchy Worries

Witchy Wishes

Saffron Diffley

Crime and Retribution

Vice and Verdict

Felonies and Penalties (Saffron Diffley Short 1)

The B-Team

Once Upon a Spy

Tate-à-Tate

Enemy of the Tates

Ghosts vs. Spies

The Ghost Who Came in from the Cold

Witchy Fingers

Witchy Trouble

Witchy Hexations

Witchy Possessions

Witchy Riches

Box Set 1 (Books 1-4)

The Mysteries of Bell & Whitehouse

One Spoonful of Trouble

Two Scoops of Murder

Three Shots of Disaster

Box Set 1 (Books 1-3)

A Twist of Wraith

A Touch of Ghost

A Clash of Spooks

Box Set 2 (Books 4-6)

The Stuffing of Nightmares

A Breath of Dead Air

An Act of Hodd

Box Set 3 (Books 7-9)

A Game of Dons

Standalone Novels

When in Bruges

The Whiskered Spy

ThrillFix

Homejacking

The Eighth Billionaire

The Wrong Woman

ABOUT NIC

Nic Saint is the pen name for writing couple Nick and Nicole Saint. They've penned 80+ novels in the romance, cat sleuth, middle grade, suspense, comedy and cozy mystery genres. Nicole has a background in accounting and Nick in political science and before being struck by the writing bug the Saints worked odd jobs around the world (including massage therapist in Mexico, gardener in Italy, restaurant manager in India, and Berlitz teacher in Belgium).

When they're not writing they enjoy Christmas-themed Hallmark movies (whether it's Christmas or not), all manner of pastry, comic books, a daily dose of yoga (to limber up those limbs), and spoiling their big red tomcat Tommy.

www.nicsaint.com

Made in the USA
Coppell, TX
22 July 2020

31486229R00152